*"Tess may lose her best friend! Will sixth g...
worst year of her life?*

Tess gasped as she faced the mirror. The circle she had drawn yesterday had been transformed into a complete face with crossed eyes and a crooked mouth. Worst of all were the huge ears with the word "Dumbo" written in one and "Flyers" in the other. Underneath someone had scrawled, "Mirror, Mirror, on the wall, who's the biggest geek of all? Tess Thomas!"

Tess turned around and grasped for a stall. The ceiling circled the stall as if in orbit, and she couldn't get a deep breath. She rested on the toilet seat. After a few minutes, the room slowed down, but hot tears still splashed her cheeks. Unlike yesterday, Tess couldn't will herself not to cry. The Coronado Club, of course! But which one drew this? Lauren? Andrea?

Then she remembered, and the memory hit her like a baseball bat in the gut. The only person who had heard her called "Dumbo Flyers" last summer was Colleen. Tess couldn't believe it. Not Colleen! Just a few weeks ago, Tess would have defended her friend to anyone, certain Colleen would have done the same for her. And now Colleen had turned on her.

Secret Sisters: (se'-krit sis'-terz) n. Two friends who choose each other to be everything a real sister should be: loyal and loving. They share with and help each other no matter what!

Secret ✳ Sisters

Heart to Heart

Sandra Byrd

WATERBROOK
PRESS

COLORADO SPRINGS

HEART TO HEART

PUBLISHED BY WATERBROOK PRESS

5446 North Academy Boulevard, Suite 200

Colorado Springs, Colorado 80918

A division of Random House, Inc.

Scriptures in the Secret Sisters series are quoted from the
International Children's Bible, New Century Version,
copyright ©1986, 1988 by Word Publishing,
Nashville, TN 37214. Used by permission.

ISBN 1-57856-229-5 (previously ISBN 1-57856-015-2)

Printed in the United States of America

1999

3 5 7 9 10 8 6 4

To my parents, John and Susan Mike,
who taught me to make good decisions.

one

There Must Be Some Mistake

Friday, August 30

The Arizona heat shimmered above the sandy desert landscape. Hot asphalt squished beneath Tess's sandals as she and her best friend, Colleen, raced up the last hill before reaching school. Today was posting day at Coronado Elementary, the day they would find out whose classes they were in.

"Everybody's crowding the hallways!" Tess said, pushing her long chestnut hair back as she headed toward the sixth-grade hall.

"I know, the little kids came with their mommies," Colleen said. "It's so babyish. I'm glad we're old enough to come alone."

She could still hear Colleen, but Tess's attention was drawn away. A young girl with pink-ribboned pigtails plopped to the floor, tripped by some eager kid racing down the main hall. "Here, let me help." Tess grabbed the girl's elbow, pulling her to her feet. The girl smiled, and then her mother came forward, clasping her daughter with relief. That taken care of, Tess scanned the hall for her friend. There she was, over by last year's class pictures.

"Hey, speed up!" Colleen called as Tess hurried toward her. "Look at my hair last year. Gross. It's better with bangs, don't you think? I can't wait until they take new pictures and toss these in the dump."

Tess was about to say how nice Colleen's hair had looked last year, too, but Colleen kept talking. "Come on, let's hit the lists! I wonder who else is in our class?" They continued down the hall toward the sixth-grade rooms, but Tess couldn't avoid glancing at her fifth-grade class picture. Her smile wilted as her eyes drew to the lonely girl standing on the edge of the crowd, hands behind her back, face downcast.

"There I am," she whispered to herself. Tears welled as she remembered the solitary lunches, reading alone at recess, watching other girls pass notes while she pretended to do her work. Worst of all, no one had ever chosen her to be science partner, and science was her best subject. Being the new girl was hard. She had ended up mismatched with other leftover kids.

"Oh, well, not this year." She blinked the moisture from her eyes and caught up with Colleen.

Nerves buzzed Tess's stomach as they approached the classroom doors. "I hope we're together."

"We will be," Colleen said. "My mom called the school to make sure I was assigned to Mr. Basil. Last year his class won the math decathlon."

"I heard that Mr. Basil doesn't read notes aloud if he

catches you passing any," Tess added. She reached his door first and scanned the list, the list that would make her day or doom her life.

"Here's your name, Colleen Clark. Right at the top with the other *C*'s."

"Yes!" Colleen said, giving Tess the thumbs up. "Check for your name."

"Terrence, Albert," Tess read aloud. "Tongue, James." She stopped, unwilling to believe what she saw. Or didn't see. She checked the list again. "You're kidding. No way! I'm not in this class?" *Thomas, Tess* did not appear on the list. She clenched her teeth.

"It's okay." Colleen circled her arm around her friend's shoulders. "Don't worry. Maybe they made a mistake. Maybe your name isn't on any list. Come on, let's check the other rooms."

Tugging on Tess's arm, Colleen dragged her to the next classroom, Ms. Froget's. Nobody wanted "The Frog." Her breath was heavy with menthol cigarettes, and she handed out pink discipline slips like reverse Valentines. She delivered at least one to each student, more to those kids she didn't really like.

"Thank goodness," sighed Tess, hastily reading the list. "No Thomases. Maybe there is a mistake." Her stomach calmed, and her heart filled with hope. She would be in Colleen's class after all.

"See, I told you we would be together. We have to," Colleen said. "Next, Ms. Martinez's room." They marched toward the last sixth-grade classroom. "You can have your mom call the school and explain that your name was left off Mr. Basil's list." Colleen reached Ms. Martinez's door first and started to read the names.

"Oh, no," she groaned. "Your name is here. This is totally bad!"

Tess gulped air before diving through the list. Sure enough, there was her name. She searched for anyone else she knew. No one.

"Don't worry. I have a plan," Colleen said.

Colleen always did. She was pretty and popular, and Tess could hardly believe her good luck when Colleen had picked her out of all the other girls on the swim team to pal up with last summer. Colleen knew everybody, and Tess hoped she would finally be popular, too.

"Go home and tell your mom to call the school," Colleen instructed. "She can insist that you *have* to be in Mr. Basil's class. They're pretty good about changing teachers if parents call. We need to be in the same class!"

"I know," Tess said. "But I don't know if my mom will call."

"Explain to her how important it is. Does she know how depressed you'll be if we're not together? Does she want you to be alone? Besides, I've been thinking we should start a club, and we have to be together for that!" Colleen stared into the window of Ms. Martinez's door, using it as a mirror. Grabbing half of her ponytail in each hand she pulled it tight, then she poofed her bangs.

"You're right . . . ," Tess mumbled.

Colleen spun around and cried out, "Lauren, you're back! How fabulous."

Tess snapped out of her daze.

"Hi." Lauren Mayfield ran up and hugged Colleen. "I'm in Mr. Basil's class, and I saw your name on the list, too! Isn't that cool?"

"Yes!" Colleen answered.

"Are you in Mr. Basil's class?" Lauren turned toward Tess.

Colleen answered for her. "No, she isn't. I mean, not yet, anyway. Her mom's going to get her in."

"Great," Lauren said, but not as if she meant it. She looked at Tess again with a prize-winning, fake smile. Tess faked a smile back at her. Unlike Tess, Colleen had had a best friend in fifth grade—Lauren. However, Lauren had been away at her grandparents' farm for most of the summer and hadn't been sure if she was coming back. At least, that's what Colleen thought. Looking at them together, Tess had the uneasy feeling that Lauren was back in more ways than one.

Lauren turned to Colleen. "Do you want to come over to swim?"

"Sure," Colleen answered. "Let's run to my house and pick up my suit." She turned toward Tess and continued, "You can come, too, if you want."

"Yeah, um, sure," Lauren muttered.

"No, thanks," Tess said. She could tell Lauren didn't want her there. "I told my mom I'd come right home, and I need to talk to her about calling the school."

"Right. Good idea." Lauren grabbed Colleen's arm to

pull her down the hall toward the front door. "Let's go! It's getting late."

"Bye, Tess. I'll call you later," Colleen promised over her shoulder as she started down the hall. Tess stood there, frozen, watching them leave. Lauren whispered something in Colleen's ear, and they both giggled.

At that moment Tess knew, she just knew, they were walking away from her forever.

First Morning

Tuesday, September 3

The alarm announced Tuesday morning much too soon. When it bleated at 7:00 A.M., Tess begged it for five more minutes. She struggled to force her eyes open but then gave up. She dozed off again.

A few minutes later a faint tapping noise awakened her as Mrs. Thomas opened the door and poked in her head. "Time to wake up, honey. I made a special breakfast. Come and eat before Tyler finishes it off." She gently shut the door.

Pushing her hair away from her face, Tess reached her hands toward the ceiling, stretched, and then slid out of bed. Oh, yeah. How could she have forgotten? The first awful day of sixth grade.

Fifteen minutes later three outfits were inside out and thrown about the room, discarded like fashion roadkill as quickly as they had been considered. The outfit she had chosen last night didn't seem right today. She wanted to wear something that would show off her

"Forever Friends" necklace, the one Colleen had given her last summer. Just in case Lauren had any doubts about who was Colleen's best friend now.

Tess went back to the dresser and yanked out the baby blue T-shirt she had purchased yesterday at Robinson's-May. After pulling it on, she smoothed her hand over her static-filled hair. "There. I guess this looks okay. I wonder what Colleen will wear." Probably something blue, too, since that was Colleen's favorite color.

Tinny music twanged, and the faithful ballerina twirled in Tess's jewelry box while she sorted through the tangled mess. Finally finding the hidden dangling earrings, she put them on. She knew dangling earrings were forbidden by her mom, but maybe that rule was for last year. Surely sixth grade was different. After retrieving the necklace from under her shirt, she abandoned the clutter to walk to the bathroom.

"Gross! Is it asking too much for Tyler to rinse out the sink after brushing his teeth?" She stared at globs of toothpaste, just like every other morning. The mornings Tyler remembered to brush his teeth, that is. How could a kid who polished his sneakers leave this mess? She ran the hot water hard, hoping the goop would wash down. It didn't. She squeezed some mint gel on her toothbrush and, after brushing, washed her face. Then she switched off the bathroom light and headed out the door.

"Wait a second!" Flicking the light back on she remembered. Lip gloss. Breaking open a new tube of Passion Fruit, she let it glide over her lips. Mmm. She kissed the mirror, leaving a slightly sticky smooch on its smooth surface. Perfect.

A minute later she slipped into her chair at the breakfast table and sipped her milk. Mrs. Thomas set a plate of fresh pancakes in front of her. They were a pleasant change from the usual yogurt. Steam rose, thickly scenting the air with plump, hot blueberries squeezed into a buttermilk robe. Tess's stomach meowed. Maybe she felt hungry after all.

"There's still time, you know," Tess started.

"Time for what, honey?" Her mom flipped a stack onto her own plate and sat down.

"To call the school. And change my class."

"Tess, we've already been over this. You were assigned to Ms. Martinez's class. She might be really nice. We don't know anything about her. Besides, I'm sure you'll make some new friends; maybe you'll even like them as much as Colleen. Try to have a positive attitude. Sulking isn't going to help." She finished her sentence and took a bite.

Tess's face fell. Didn't her mom understand? Not if she could say things like "positive attitude."

Fear and anxiety bubbled until Tess burst out, "I am positive I'm not changing any attitude until you call the school!" Her lips quivered.

"Watch your tone, miss," Mom said.

"You don't understand. You're ruining my life!" Tess wailed as she stood back from the table.

Tyler glanced up from his meal. "Girls. Never could understand them. Glad I don't have to." He plucked a cricket from an old margarine container hidden on the

floor and lifted the top off his horned toad's cage, drop-
ping the tasty tidbit in. Hercules gobbled it up. "No
need for you to go hungry, old boy," Tyler said, mim-
icking the accent he heard on the British mystery tele-
vision shows he watched.

Sickened by the bug's death on top of everything
else, Tess fled the room running down the hall to her
bedroom. Once in her room she flopped onto her bed.
How could she face this day? This year? She heard a
light knock on her door. She sat there for a moment,
glancing at the clock before answering. Her clock
glared "7:45" at her in bold red numerals.

"Yes?" she called.

"Come on, honey. I do understand. And I'll give you
a ride so you won't be late." Mom's steps softened as
she pattered back down the hall.

"Maybe it won't be so bad," Tess said to her reflection, slowly straightening her shirt in front of her oval,
full-length mirror. "Maybe Lauren will find another
friend." Grabbing her backpack, she was off to join her
mom and Ty in the car.

"Hey, I thought it was my turn to sit in the front."
Tess opened one of the back doors. She climbed in and
buckled up as Tyler turned around to face her.

"Too bad, you lose," he said, forming the letter *L* with
his thumb and fingers and placing it against his forehead to signal "Loser."

Impossible, Tess thought, rolling her eyes, *to live with
an eight-year-old boy. I'd much rather have had a sister.*

Scrunch. The bottom of the car scraped the sidewalk.
Her mom always backed out too fast. Two minutes

later they swooped into the school parking lot, a lone eagle landing among flocks of hawks.

The car lurched as Mrs. Thomas pulled in and then slammed on the brakes. Tess crouched down in her seat, hoping no one saw the car screech to a halt. She sat up as Tyler bounded out of the car.

Her mom cleared her throat and held out her hand toward Tess.

"What?" Tess asked.

"The earrings. They dangle."

"Oh, Mom, come on." Even as Tess said it, she unclasped the earrings, handing them to her mother. Obviously her mom didn't think being in sixth grade made any difference. Dutifully, Tess brushed a kiss on her mother's cheek and turned to go.

"I love you, Tess," her mom called after her. "Make it a great day."

three

New Year,
Old Feelings

Tuesday, September 3

The motto YOU ARE BECOMING WHO YOU ARE TO BE was engraved in smooth stone above the main door to the stuccoed school. Tess stared at it for a minute before heading toward the sixth-grade hallway, hanging around to see if she could catch Colleen. After a few minutes passed with no sign of her friend, she slouched into class.

She was one of the first to arrive. As she put away her supplies, she heard someone ask, "Is anyone sitting here?"

Tess looked up at a girl with French-braided hair the color of caramel syrup. The girl motioned toward the desk next to Tess.

"No, uh, I don't think so," Tess answered. The girl set her backpack on the desk and opened it up. Tess finished arranging her things and closed her desk.

A tube of the girl's lip gloss dropped to the floor, and

she bent over to retrieve it. "What flavor is that?" Tess blurted before she could stop herself.

"Mango. This is the first year I can wear it to school," the girl answered. She didn't seem to mind the question. "I really like the scent. It reminds me of the trip we took to Hawaii last year." When the girl smiled, her whole face looked happy, not just her mouth. Cool. Real. Not faked, like Lauren's.

Tess said, "This is the first year I can wear lip gloss to school, too. Mine's Passion Fruit." She glanced at a picture the girl was taping to the inside of her desk. "Is that your horse?"

"Yeah, I have two horses. I mean, my grandparents have horses at their house in Gilbert. They seem like my horses, though, because I like them better than anyone else does. I mostly ride the two youngest, Dustbuster and Solomon."

"I like horses. Only I don't get to ride much. My mom took me to Tapatio Stables once."

An awkward moment passed before the girl smiled at Tess again, then turned back to her desk.

The first bell rang, signaling Ms. Martinez to call the class to order. She was young. And she had a 3-D solar system model in the science corner. This might be okay.

"My name is Erin," the girl across the aisle whispered.

"My name is Tess," she replied softly, as Ms. Martinez gave her opening day introduction. The Pledge of Allegiance crackled on the intercom, and the school year began.

An hour later Tess decided she needed a drink of water. On the way she would peek into Mr. Basil's class to get Colleen's attention. Maybe Colleen could get a drink, too, and the two of them could make a plan to meet at recess and lunch. Once in the hall, Tess buzzed directly to Mr. Basil's class.

His back was turned, and as Tess scanned the class, her eyes rested uncomfortably on a group surrounding Colleen . . . and Lauren. With their desks side by side they looked a little too cozy. After a moment of longing, Tess returned to her classroom, forgetting about the drink of water. She would have to do something about this. This year was not going to be the fifth grade all over again.

four

Squaw Peak

Thursday, September 5

Two nights later was hiking night, a special time almost every week when Tess and her dad were together. As usual, her father reached the top of Squaw Peak first. Like the chubby finger of a demanding baby, Squaw Peak jutted out from the mostly flat palm of the Phoenix landscape. From a distance, the mountain looked smooth and steep. Close up, though, crumbling rocks, cracks, crevices, and the beaten path from thousands of hikers who climbed this trail each year came into focus.

Tess's dad chose a smooth rock to sit down on before taking off his glasses. Pulling a small towel out of his fanny pack, he wiped the sweat from his glasses and then from his forehead before putting the glasses back on. Tess sat down next to him and guzzled a long drink from her water bottle.

In fact, Tess and her dad had climbed this trail dozens of times. He felt exercise was good for the soul and built a competitive spirit; so he made sure the family got plenty of it. Tess loved hiking and usually her father's company. Most of all she enjoyed the watercolor sunset as dusk filtered through layers of desert dust. Evening light bathed the mountain, warming the stubborn little shrubs clinging to its nooks and crannies.

"What's up?" Her dad broke the silence.

"What do you mean?"

"Well, Mom says you've been sassy the last few days, short-tempered. That's not like you. You're usually defender of the downtrodden, sunshine for the sadhearted."

"Dad . . . ," Tess rolled her eyes at the exaggeration. Sometimes she felt uncomfortable talking about her private thoughts, especially with her dad. But anxiety about school boiled over, spilling out in words. "I feel totally left out. I finally have a best friend and a really good chance to be in the popular group. But now, since I'm not in Colleen's class, I'm afraid I won't have any friends at all!" Her face flushed with heat and embarrassment.

Her dad clasped her shoulder. "I'm sorry to hear it." Tess could tell by the look on his face that he didn't get it. "I'm sure you'll be okay. You're strong. You'll make some new friends. Quit worrying about it; do something! There's always hope, even when things seem darkest. Remember," he said as he stood up, motioning for her to start down the trail, "it's not always about getting the best situations, instead—"

"Do the best you can with the situation you have."

Tess finished the thought with a sigh. She had heard that line at least sixty-six times.

What did he expect her to do with this situation? Maybe he could just brush it off, but Tess couldn't. Her dad meant well; yet he obviously didn't understand how major it was to have friends. Popular friends. Any friends, actually, besides the ones at her old school, whom she hardly ever talked to anymore.

It had been more than a year since she had moved. Her parents had thought moving would be a good thing—nice schools and close to everything. But it hadn't worked out that way for Tess. Instead, she had spent the entire fifth grade wondering if her old friends even remembered her, since she didn't have any new ones.

Until Colleen, that is. Colleen had included her in everything, introducing her to important people. It was a miracle they had met on swim team. How lucky Tess was to be picked by Colleen. Colleen cared about Tess. What was her dad thinking? What should she hope for?

"Now that we have that settled, I hope you'll be civil to your mother. Okay?" Her father waited for an answer, and after Tess nodded in agreement, he turned back toward the trail.

It wasn't really settled, but her heart ached at the possibility that she had hurt her mom's feelings. Her mother could get on her nerves, but Tess loved her. She was the best mother around. Tess promised herself she would do better. She hated to hurt anyone's feelings; she knew how that felt.

"Hey, Dad," Tess called as she scooted past him. She raced a few steps ahead on the trail before calling over her shoulder, "Last one to the car is a brown banana. Do I need to remind you who was the brown banana last week?"

He chuckled, stepping up his pace a little too late.

✻

"What are you doing in here?" Tess tossed her shoes into the closet as she stepped into her room.

"Mom said I could use your computer to finish my homework. I wish I had one of my own." The computer beeped as Tyler exited through a myriad of screens to close down his work.

"Yeah, well, maybe next year. I had to wait until Mom bought a new one for work. Next time she buys one, you can have this, and I'll take the one she has now."

"You stink," Tyler said. "I really mean it, old girl. Stinkus amongus. Perhaps you should visit the W.C. and tidy up."

"Can you lay off that English accent? And what is Hercules doing in here?" Tess tapped the side of the toad's cage. She might be more favorably inclined toward Hercules if he weren't always devouring helpless bugs.

"Mom was banging around in the kitchen tonight, and he got scared and shot blood at her through his eyes. It hit the glass, but Mom got mad and said he had to stay out of the kitchen. So he'll bunk with me from now on." Tyler grabbed the cage on the way to his room.

Tess walked over to shut off her computer then

changed her mind, logging into her "Hidden Treasures" program.

Dear Diary,

I'm worried this may be the worst year of my life. I am not kidding or exaggerating. This is supposed to be my best grade, the one in which I am a boss of the school before I start middle school, but too bad for me. Everyone I know is in Mr. Basil's class, except for one girl I just met. She, Erin I mean, is okay, but she's not Colleen. Don't you think I deserve to have friends, Diary? I've worked hard to be popular. Lauren is trying to take Colleen away from me. I just know it. The worst part is I have no one to talk to except a stupid diary. No offense. Mom would never understand. She would tell me, "Make new friends and keep the old. One is silver and the other's gold" or something else silly.

I tried to talk with Dad tonight, but it went right over his head. He always thinks it will be okay. He says there's hope, but what hope could there be?

Hey! I just remembered the club, the club that Colleen said we're going to start. If we start it right away, we can get totally involved in that together! I'll remind her of it tomorrow. Maybe Dad's right. Maybe hope is coming. I wish you were real, Diary. I wish you could talk and help me, tell me what to do. But of course you can't. Good night, Diary.

Love, Tess
P.S. Ms. Martinez seems pretty good so far. I'll give you an update later.

five ✳

Coronado Club

Friday, September 6

Tess fidgeted, trying to pass the time until lunch so she could get Colleen by herself and talk about starting the club. "Sixth graders, please return to your seats," Ms. Martinez instructed at the end of free time. Except for the clock's loud ticking, the room grew quiet.

"The district is sponsoring a science contest, open to every sixth-grade class in Scottsdale," Ms. Martinez continued. "The winning class will earn a field trip to the planetarium in Tucson with a lunch stop at McDonald's. I love the planetarium, so I want us to win! Your first assignment is to write a proposal on what you think the class should submit as our project. Submissions are due in one week. I'll review them all before choosing one. The class will work together on the project, and we'll turn it in by the end of October. The winning class will be announced right before Thanksgiving. I'm sure we can win, if we work hard. After all, we are the smartest class, right?" Ms.

Martinez winked. "I'll give final instructions after lunch."

She returned to the board, erasing the last lesson before writing out math problems. Chalk dust floated through the air, and the escaping powder tickled Tess's nose.

From her seat next to Tess, Erin passed a note. "Have you ever been to the planetarium? Circle one: Yes No"

Tess opened her desk slightly so she could read the note without being seen. She circled "No," then wrote: "It sounds fun. A day without school sounds fun, too. So does lunch at McDonald's. I hope we win. I like your hair braided that way. Do you do it yourself?"

She dropped the note on the floor between their desks. Erin reached down to pick it up and returned: "Yes. I can do yours, too, if you want. It would look great."

"No thanks," wrote Tess. She chewed her pencil eraser for a minute before adding, "I don't pull my hair back." She didn't explain that at the Y swim team this past summer a boy had taken one look at her ears and called them "Dumbo Flyers." Everyone, absolutely everyone, laughed. Even Colleen. Afterward, Tess vowed she would never pull her hair back again. She held the note under her palm, securing it with her thumb, and slipped it back. Ms. Martinez looked up with a stern expression, as if to say "No more notes" just before the lunch bell rang.

Kangaroo meat again. At least the rumor said it was kangaroo meat chopped up inside the stroganoff.

That's sure what it smelled like. Tess watched as the lunchroom workers slopped food onto her neon tray that was beat up enough to have been here since Colonel Scott founded the city. At least the fries looked good, and the salad did, too. Tess waited in line with the others for dessert, grabbing some silverware and a carton of skim milk.

Colleen strode in, and the kid behind Tess let Colleen cut in. "Hi, how's old Martinez doing?"

"Not bad," Tess answered, smiling. "And she's not old. She just graduated from college."

"Oh," said Colleen, looking around. "Well, what I really came to tell you is that I started the club. It's called the Coronado Club. It's only for cool sixth graders. Like you, of course. Lauren's already in. I talked to her yesterday. We can't wait for you to be a member, too."

"Great," Tess said, perking up. She wasn't going to be left out after all. "It's so amazing how we think alike! I was going to ask you about the club today. Why don't you tell me more at the table?"

"Well," Colleen shifted her weight between her feet, staring at the ground. "That's the problem. We decided our table would only be for active club members. You're going to be a member, of course, after you're initiated. But you're not a member yet; so you can't sit with us today."

"What do you mean, 'initiated'? You're my best friend!"

"I know, but each member has to do something important to prove her loyalty to the others," Colleen insisted, looking Tess in the eye. "Of course, we know you're loyal. It won't be a problem. I'll talk to the others today and ask them what your initiation will be. I'll call you over the weekend, okay?"

"Well, I guess so," Tess answered, even though it wasn't. "I thought maybe we could do something together this weekend."

"I'm sorry. I already have plans. Maybe next weekend? I'll call you Sunday." Colleen squeezed Tess's arm, then cut out of line, walking back to stand with Lauren.

Tess walked through the lunchroom, finally sitting down at a table toward the middle. *Prove my loyalty to who? What is going on?* Colleen never left Tess out. Tess needed Colleen, and Colleen needed Tess. Right? She glanced over at the table where Colleen and Lauren sat. Melody Shirowsky sat with them, pushing her sleeves up her long, slender arms and flashing her dimpled smile. Everyone thought Melody was the prettiest girl in sixth grade. Getting mad now, Tess wondered if Melody had to be initiated or if she was cute enough to be in automatically.

"Hey, can I sit here?"

Tess looked up to see it was Erin.

"Sure," she answered, still upset. "Go ahead." She wondered if Erin thought it was weird that Tess sat alone. Erin must have noticed Tess usually sat with Colleen. Tess hoped people wouldn't think she was a geek or anything.

"I brought some more pictures of my horses. Oh, I mean my grandparents' horses. I wondered if you want to see them." Erin pulled out an envelope thick with pictures.

"Okay."

Erin unstuck the envelope and handed the photos over one by one. "This one is Dustbuster. Whenever she runs, she kicks up a lot of dust. She's a quarter horse with a real good personality. She loves carrots. And guess what? She'll only eat them if they've been peeled!" Erin giggled as she passed the next picture along. Tess's anger was forgotten for now, and she giggled back.

"This one is named Solomon because he is wise. He can tell if his rider is new or experienced. He is gentle with an inexperienced rider but gives a trained rider a wild ride." Erin passed across a few more photos. Tess noticed a cute boy in one but was too embarrassed to ask who he was.

"These are great, Erin. Thanks for showing me." Tess finished her lunch and asked, "Where's Jessica?" Erin usually sat with Jessica Blessing, her best friend, who was in The Frog's class.

"In Seattle," Erin mumbled.

Tess decided not to press for details. "Do you want to go outside?" Tess asked. She figured that was better than sitting in the lunchroom alone.

"Okay." Erin crumpled her napkin into a ball and piled the rest of her trash onto the tray. "Let's go."

Tess followed her to the garbage can where they cleared their trays. The usually noisy lunchroom was quiet. Almost everyone had escaped into the hot noon sunshine. Tess wondered what Colleen would think of Erin and whether Colleen liked horses. Funny, even though Colleen was Tess's best friend, Tess didn't know a lot about her.

six

Initiation

Sunday, September 8

After a boring weekend of yard work with "General Dad" giving orders and no help from lazy "Lieutenant Tyler," Tess couldn't wait for Colleen's call. It finally came.

"I bought a new outfit this weekend," Colleen said.

"Really?" Tess cradled the phone between her shoulder and her ear. "What's it like?"

"It's a black sweater dress with a jazzy black velvet hat. I can't wait to wear it. Also, I bought some new Cheri shampoo, the kind that washes a tint into your hair. I finally convinced my mom I'm old enough to try it. Oh, yeah, I'll bring your book back to school this week. Thanks for loaning it to me."

"No problem," Tess answered. She sat on the floor folding a big pile of her clothes while she talked. "Where did you buy the shampoo?"

"At Pay Less-Save More," Colleen answered. "That reminds me. Your mom almost ran over my mom in the parking lot last week. I heard my mom tell my dad that Molly Thomas needs driving lessons before she kills someone."

A hot flush rose from Tess's neck to her forehead, prickling her hair. Colleen's mom, of all people.

"Sorry," Tess said. "Tyler was probably distracting her." Tess moved on to another stack of clothes and changed ears. Her left ear throbbed from holding the phone.

"Well, that's not why I called," Colleen continued. "I talked with the other club members, and we've decided on your initiation."

Tess stopped folding clothes; a funny tingle danced in her stomach.

"Well—"

Just then Tess heard heavy breathing on the phone. Panting, actually. She interrupted. "Colleen, are you breathing heavily?"

"What?" Colleen sounded confused.

Boyish giggling broke out.

"Mom! Tyler's listening in on my phone call!" Tess shouted down the hall to her mother's office. This was totally embarrassing. Now they could hear Tyler's friend Big Al belch a big, juicy burp on the line. Gross! Big Al was always eating, so Big Al was always burping. He would even say "hello" with a burp when Tess opened the front door. And his burps usually smelled like hot dogs.

"Tyler, hang up the phone. It's time for Al to go home. Now!" her dad hollered down the hallway. The other line clicked off.

"I'm really sorry, Colleen," Tess said. "I'm sure it was Big Al's idea."

"Yeah, sure. Well, what I was saying is the club has decided that for your initiation you have to trip Unibrow as she takes her tray to her lunch table this Friday."

"What do you mean?" Tess asked. "Who's Unibrow?"

"You mean you don't know who Unibrow is? You're out of it, Tess. I can see I'm going to have to clue you in. Do you know Marcia Porcetti?" Colleen asked.

"Yeah, I think so. Is she Unibrow?"

"Yes," Colleen confirmed. "Haven't you noticed her eyebrows? She's so hairy her eyebrows practically connect. It's disgusting. You can't tell where one brow begins and the other ends. So she's a unibrow. And her arms are hairy, too. She's like an ape. Anyway, she's always one of the last people into the lunchroom. Here's the plan. Friday sit at the very end of the table. Then, when Marcia walks by, stick out your foot and trip her. Everyone will laugh hysterically. Okay?"

Now Tess's stomach was a big blob of bread dough that was being squeezed, punched, and kneaded. "I don't even know Marcia," Tess replied. "I don't want to hurt her feelings. And I might get in trouble. Can't I do something else?"

" 'Fraid not," Colleen said. "That's what we decided. Don't worry. Come on, Tess. Andrea Blackstone is dying to be a member, and Lauren wants her to join next. But I want you."

"Andrea!" Tess said. "She doesn't even like to hang out with girls. She would rather play touch football with the guys."

"Well," Colleen said, "she wants in."

A minute later Tess agreed. "Okay, I guess I'll do it. Friday?"

"Right!" Colleen said with enthusiasm. "I knew I could count on you. It's going to be great to have you in the club. I've missed you, Tess. Friday night we're having a party—with boys—at Lauren's house. Then the next week we're having a major mall crawl. It'll be great. See you next Friday!"

"Should I call you before then?" Tess asked.

"Um, I think it would be better if we wait until after the initiation. You know how it goes. Okay?"

"Okay," Tess said weakly. "See you." She hung up the phone. This was worse than she had expected. Walking to her mirror, she pulled it close to her face and stared at her eyebrows. "I don't even know Marcia," she said, wrinkling her forehead. "And I never noticed her eyebrows." Something besides the initiation bugged Tess, nagged at the back of her brain. What was it? Something about Colleen and Marcia and herself, but she couldn't figure out exactly what.

Stepping away from the mirror, she plopped down on the floor. "Oh, well, it'll be okay," she reassured herself. "I deserve to be in the popular group. Marcia isn't my friend. The only friend I really have is Colleen."

Tess stood up, smiling, remembering that Colleen had said she missed Tess. Tess missed Colleen, too. It would be good to be together again. A light rap sounded on her door.

"May I come in?" Tess's mother stepped into her room.

Tess noticed again how pretty her mom was. Her eyes were the color of summer ivy, and her face was peach-smooth like Tess's. Except her mom had tiny lines here and there, etched through thirty-six years of smiling. Tess was proud of her mom but a little embarrassed when she remembered what Mrs. Clark had said about her driving. "Come on in," Tess said.

"I thought you could use some help cleaning your room." Her mom bent over a pile of newly folded clothes and picked them up. After walking to the dresser, she opened one of the drawers and placed the clothes inside.

"Thanks, Mom," Tess said with relief. "I can use the help. It's a mess again." She walked over to her desk and began to sort through papers.

"Are you okay? You look pale." Mom headed toward the closet and sat down on the floor to straighten out Tess's shoes.

"Yeah, I'm okay," she answered, tossing math scratch papers into the trash can.

"I'm sorry about Tyler on the phone," Mom said. "Dad had a long talk with him, and he lost TV privileges for two days."

"It's okay. It was Colleen."

"How's she doing? Is she enjoying Mr. Basil's class?"

"I think so," Tess answered. "We haven't talked much this past week. We keep playing phone tag." She brightened. "We should be spending more time together soon, though. Colleen started a club and asked me to join. It's called the Coronado Club."

"That's nice. Maybe you can have a club meeting

here someday." Finished with the shoes, she moved to the stereo to stack Tess's CDs.

"Good idea," said Tess. "Thanks."

"I think we're just about finished in here. Why don't you take a shower now so you don't have to get up early?" Mom straightened the bookshelf, then hands on hips, surveyed the room. "This room looks great, Tess. I didn't think I would like the pattern you chose, but now I think you were right. The curtains and spread are cheery and positive, like my girl. Better get into the shower." She ruffled Tess's hair before leaving the room.

Tess ambled toward her closet to get her robe. Maybe she should have mentioned the initiation. But she knew her mom wouldn't approve, and Tess didn't want to disappoint her. Of course, she didn't want to disappoint Colleen either.

seven

Party Invitation

Tuesday, September 10

Monday cruised by, and soon Tuesday was half over. Although Tess was busy reading at her desk, she knew Ms. Martinez had come back into the room because a gentle scent floated lightly through the air. Tess wondered what kind of perfume Ms. M. wore. It smelled like the lilac bush in Grandma Kate's backyard. Closing her novel, Tess waited for afternoon class to start.

"Okay, sixth graders, please take out your social studies books and open to chapter two. Brian, would you read the first section aloud?"

Brian Goldstein stumbled through the passage while Tess watched her teacher. Ms. Martinez's shiny, almost-black hair tumbled down like a molasses waterfall. She wore it pulled back with a large silver-and-turquoise clip. Yesterday, when they had studied immigration, Ms. Martinez had told the class her parents had come to the United States from Mexico twenty-five years ago. They had worked for twenty years doing odd jobs and growing chili peppers in New Mexico until they could afford to buy their own little farm. Ms. Martinez had won a scholarship to Arizona State University; that's how she had become a teacher. She had promised them they would have a Mexico party some day this year.

Brian had finished, and Selinda read now. "Uh-hmm." Tess heard Erin clear her throat and looked over as Erin dropped a note on the floor.

"I know this is sort of late, but do you want to come to my birthday party on Saturday? Circle one: Yes No Maybe"

Tess chewed on the end of her pen, thinking for a minute before circling "Yes." It probably wouldn't be as much fun as Colleen's sleepover party last summer, but it might be fun to ride horses. Since it wouldn't interfere with Lauren's party on Friday night, why not? Tess wrote to the side of the check mark, "If my mom lets me. Where do you live?" She slid the note across the aisle.

Erin pulled a new piece of paper from her notebook and wrote, "I live in Paradise Valley, but my party is at my grandparents' in Gilbert. I'll give you the invitation at lunch."

"Okay," mouthed Tess.

"Well, Tess, are you going to read this section or just what's passed across the aisle?" Ms. Martinez interrupted. She stared at the note until Erin slipped it into her pocket.

"Uh, yes. Sure," Tess answered. "I mean, where are we?"

"Section three."

Tess cleared her throat. "By now the wagon trains had reached the Oregon Territory. . . ." After Tess finished reading the section, the class put away its books and herded to the front of the room to work with maps and computers.

"That was a close one!" Tess breathed to Erin.

"I know. We were almost busted!" Erin replied. "I have an idea. Let's sign our notes with our lip gloss names so if they are intercepted no one will know which of us wrote what."

"Good idea, Mango," said Passion Fruit. "We could seal the notes with a smudge of lip gloss, too. Just for extra protection."

Erin giggled. "I'm glad you're coming to my party."

"A computer opened up," Tess said, glancing at the computer corner. "I think I'll go over there and work for a while."

"Okay," Erin headed back toward her desk.

Ms. Martinez came up behind Tess, tapping lightly on her screen. "What are you working on?" she asked with a smile, as if to let Tess know all was forgiven regarding the note.

"My geography project. After you talked to us yesterday, I decided to pick Mexico for my country report. It sounded so romantic." Tess blushed, but Ms. M. beamed.

"Well, let me know if I can loan you any books," she said, turning to talk with a student at the next computer. A gentle current of scented air trailed after her as she turned. Silver balls hooped with thin rings swung from her earlobes, tucking into her hair like tiny Saturns deep in a night sky. Once again Tess thought how sophisticated dangling earrings were. She couldn't wait to wear some. She would buy some like Ms. M.'s.

The lunch bell clanged loudly, and the class walked down the hall to the lunchroom. Tess stood in line behind Erin and Jessica. Tater tots, her favorite, were being served. Tess squirted some ketchup onto her tray as the smell of the crispy potatoes mingled with that of her plump hot dog. She plopped into the first open chair, and Erin sat next to her, handing her an invitation with directions to Erin's grandparents' house.

"Who else is coming?"

"Not very many people," admitted Erin. "My mom, my brothers, my cousins, and Jessica, of course. My dad will try to make it, if he's not working. He's a chef and has to work a lot."

"It sounds fun. Are we going to ride your horses?"

"Of course," Erin said. "That's why I'm having it in Gilbert. You can ride Solomon. He'll go easy on you."

Tess smiled; Erin was okay. When Tess glanced over at the Coronado Club table, she saw Colleen, Lauren, and Melody with their heads together. Whispering secrets, she supposed. Tess comforted herself that she would be sitting with them next week. Maybe once she was in the club, she would ask Erin and Jessica to join, too.

✳

A few minutes after Tess finished her after-school snack, she heard, "If I may say so, old girl, you are looking splendiferous today!" Tyler rambled into the room, clutching Hercules' cage while Tess tried on the new hiking shoes Dad had bought her.

"Yeah, and what do you want, Inspector?" Tess responded, knowing his compliments didn't come easily.

"The good lady, our mother, said you would be pleased to let me finish my computer game."

"Well, I'm not pleased about it, but if the good lady, our mother, said so, I suppose I'll let you." Tess tapped on Hercules' cage. "What's up, lizard lips?" Hercules sulked in the cage's corner, innately knowing friend and foe.

"Why didn't you get a dog or something?" Tess asked. "Say, speaking of dogs, where's Big Al today? Does he talk British, too?"

"No, he burps British!" Tyler burst out laughing, back to good old American English again. "Why don't you like Big Al? He's all right once you get to know him."

"No, thanks," Tess said. "I have better taste in friends."

Tyler looked at her for a long moment, then turned to the computer. Tess knew what he was thinking. Where were Tess's friends? Big Al might be rude, but he was loyal to Tyler no matter what. Everyone in the family had figured out that the friendship between Colleen and Tess had cooled; they used to talk on the phone every night. Yesterday her mom had said, "Well, you know, Lauren was Colleen's friend for years before you met her," as if to give Tess an excuse. She didn't want an excuse. She wanted a friend.

"No, Mom, you just don't get it." Tess had stormed out of the room. Inside, though, she was afraid that her mom did get it. Maybe Tess had been a convenient friend while Lauren was gone but now . . .

Tess willed the thought out of her mind. Friday was only two days away.

eight

Dear God

Thursday, September 12

Thursday was unusually hot, and after school Tess hung out by the pool, cooling off and listening to music.

Her mom opened the kitchen window and called, "I could use a little help. Would you please come in and put away these groceries?"

"Sure," Tess answered, raising herself from the pool and dripping onto the adjoining patio. The cool water sparkled and shimmered as it slapped against the azure tiles. Tess toweled off lightly, but it wasn't really necessary. The heat would have done the job in less than five minutes. Although it seemed like a luxury to people in other parts of the country, having a pool was nearly a necessity to survive scorching Arizona summers. Almost everyone had one.

The old sliding glass door squeaked its protest as Tess pulled it open, entering the family room. She pulled on her shorts and T-shirt before walking into the kitchen. Seven or eight grocery bags lined the countertops.

"Let's see if you bought anything good," Tess said, more to herself than to her mother. "Hey, chocolate chips!"

"For baking, not eating," warned Mrs. Thomas as Tess started to rip open the bag. "We can bake some cookies later tonight, if you want."

"Okay," Tess said. "What's for dinner?"

"Stir-fry. Want to help?"

"Sure, as long as I don't have to chop the veggies."

Tess's mom tossed the bag of long-grain brown rice toward her and motioned toward the rice steamer. "How is school going? You haven't said much this week."

"All right," Tess answered, running a steady stream of water from the tap into the steamer. "Actually, Ms. Martinez is turning out to be okay. She likes science. Oh, yeah, Erin invited me to her birthday party this weekend."

"Who's Erin? You haven't mentioned her before."

"She sits next to me. I met her last week." Tess said. "Her grandparents have horses in Gilbert, and she's having a few people over to ride this Saturday for her birthday. She's pretty nice. Think I can go?"

"I'll call her mom this evening for the details," Mom answered. "Jot her number down by the phone for me."

Tess fished the invitation out of her pocket. "It's on this. I'll set it on the counter. I need to get to my homework before dinner. It's hard to get it done on hiking nights."

"Okay, honey," her mom said. "Thanks for starting the rice."

Tess turned a cartwheel in the hall to the bedrooms. She shut her door and slipped on her headphones. She worked better with music. Opening up the book *Viva Mexico,* she started to research her report.

After dinner, Tess and her dad headed for Camelback Mountain. She loved to hike Camelback; it was a tough climb, but the view from the top was spectacular. Last summer, after staying in Minnesota with her grand-parents, the first thing she recognized from the air on the flight home was Camelback. Its rocky humps slumped over the desert like a tired camel that had stopped for a rest in the middle of the city. Tess reached the top seconds before her dad.

"You're doing well, Tess," he said after catching his breath. A moment later he continued, "I have an idea. My company is sponsoring a Grand Canyon Rim-to-Rim hike next May. We start the hike early, about 4:00 A.M., on a Saturday and walk from the South Rim all the way to the North Rim by dinnertime. Mom and Tyler could drive up with us, drop us off, then drive to the North Rim to meet us. It's a long hike and a chal-lenging one, but I think you can do it. What do you say? Friday is the registration. Should I sign us up?"

"Wow, all the way across the Grand Canyon? I'm not sure." Tess saw her father's jaw harden, if only slightly. After a minute she said, "It sounds hard, Dad, but I think I can do it. We have lots of time to practice." His face relaxed.

"Not practice," he said with a smile, "train! I know

you can do anything you put your mind to. I'll sign us up tomorrow." He sat back, taking a long drink of water.

Oh, yeah. Tomorrow was Friday. She had forgotten about Friday . . . and Marcia. *Dad thinks I can do anything? If only he knew.* The evening breeze chilled the sweat on her face.

"Tess," he said a few minutes later, "this is the third time I've called you. Are you okay?"

"Yeah, I'm okay. Let's start down now," she answered, stuffing her water bottle into her hiking belt and heading toward the trail. Her dad followed close behind.

"Hey, wait for me!"

Tess shuffled down the path, watching the city lights wink knowingly at each other as the daylight dimmed. Somewhere on the purple mountain a bird called to its mate. It sounded like "Cluck, cluck, cluck. So sad. So sad."

Later that night Tess crawled under the covers, pulling them up to her neck. Her bed normally felt cozy, but tonight she twisted and turned, punching her pillow in a vain attempt to get comfortable. A series of brief raps sounded on her door.

"Yes?"

"It's me—Mom."

"Come in," Tess said. A beam of light angled into the dark room as her mom opened the door. She high-stepped over piles of clothes and books to squeeze by the foot of the bed.

"Want a cookie?" Her mother held out a plate with

several fresh samples. "I know you were too tired to bake them, but I thought you might not be too tired to eat one."

The rich vanilla smell invited Tess to take a cookie, and she did. So did her mom. The cookies were warm, the chocolate chips melted. Mrs. Thomas swallowed her last bite and said, "You were sort of quiet tonight. You don't have to do the Rim-to-Rim, you know. Sometimes your father seems to expect a lot of you, but he just wants you to be the best you can be. We thought you might enjoy it, but Dad will have fun if he goes with the guys from work. Should I tell him not to sign you up?"

"No, I really do want to go. That's not it. I'm just . . ." Tess paused, wishing she could tell her mom about tomorrow. But she couldn't. ". . . just tired. I'm sure I'll feel better tomorrow."

"Okay, honey." Her mother smoothed the covers. "I talked to Erin's mom tonight. Everything is set for Saturday. They will drive you out, and I'll pick you up."

"Great," Tess said, cheering up a bit. "Thanks, Mom."

"Good night, sweetheart." She kissed Tess's forehead. "See you tomorrow. I love you."

"I love you, too," Tess answered, as her mother softly pulled the door shut behind her. Tess wished she could have shared her worries with her mom, but, well, she couldn't. She had no one at all to share with. She hadn't even wanted to write in her diary tonight. Balling up her pillow with her fists, she rolled on her side, trying to get comfortable.

Why not pray? she thought. She didn't know much about God, but Janelle, her sometime baby-sitter, said she prayed whenever she needed help. At this point, anything was worth a try.

"Dear God," Tess began, whispering under her covers. "I don't know if that's how I'm supposed to start out, but I don't have any other ideas. Can you hear me? Are you real? Janelle thinks you are. Anyway, I'm supposed to trip Marcia tomorrow, and I'm afraid. I might get in trouble. Besides, I don't even know her, and she might get hurt. But Colleen is my very best friend, if Lauren hasn't stolen her away, that is. If you really can see everything, you know that I had no friends last year. Remember? And I don't want to lose Colleen. I'm not sure what to do."

Tess listened for a voice to answer, but none came. Her body relaxed, though, finally finding a comfortable position in bed. Calm settled around her, and she grew drowsy. Two crickets chirped a rhythmic lullaby outside her bedroom window as she slipped into sleep.

nine

Lunchroom Mess

Friday, September 13

Nothing was calm, however, about Friday's lunch. Tess's clammy fists unclenched long enough to grab a lunch tray from the stack. She balanced her tray on the rail and urged it down the line toward the food. A cool piece of metal flexed against her neck. The necklace, she remembered. She recalled the day last July when Colleen had given it to her.

"Here," Colleen had said, "I brought this back from my trip to San Diego. I saw it in an open market. Right away I knew I had to buy it for you." Colleen had placed the gift into Tess's hand. Tess loved the delicate chain with a charm on it that said "Forever Friends." Immediately she had clasped it around her and hadn't taken it off since.

Now, in the lunchroom, the necklace felt more like a choke collar than a filigree chain. "Chicken nuggets or spaghetti?" the lunch lady barked.

"Uh, chicken, I guess."

"What kind of sauce? Barbecue, honey, ranch?" the lunch lady continued. Too many choices.

"Oh, I don't care. Ranch." Tess moved down the aisle, placing a shivering cherry Jell-O on her tray.

As one of the first in the lunchroom, she had her pick of tables. She chose one a few tables back and sat at the end as Colleen had instructed. She settled her tray on the table and stared wistfully down the aisle. *Next week,* she psyched herself, *I'll be sitting at the Coronado Club table with all my friends.* She poked at the chicken with her fork but didn't eat any.

"Hi," Erin said as she sat across from Tess. "New table?"

Erin! Why is she sitting here today? Where's Jessica? Doesn't she usually sit with Jessica? Erin had only sat with Tess a couple of other times. Tess scanned the lunchroom, hoping Marcia hadn't come to school today. Her heart sank. There Marcia stood, at the end of the line. Crumb!

"Oh, change of pace, I guess," Tess responded stickily. Her mouth was dry from fear. Then she remembered something. "Do you know today is Friday the thirteenth? Pretty freaky." She glanced at the lunch line. Marcia was coming closer.

Erin had food in her mouth so she didn't answer right away. The smell of the fried chicken made Tess sick to her stomach. She pushed her tray back. When she glanced at the Coronado Club table, she saw that Colleen and the others were already sitting down. Colleen shot Tess a smile, giving her a "thumbs up."

"I don't believe in Friday the thirteenth," Erin finally answered.

"You don't? Do you believe in any bad luck? Or good luck?"

"No, I don't believe in superstitions. I believe in God." Erin dunked another chicken nugget in her barbecue sauce. "Do you mind if I eat your chicken? If you're not going to, I mean."

"Go ahead," Tess answered. *How does she stay skinny when she eats so much?*

Tess scanned the lunch line. Marcia was heading down the row toward her. It seemed as if no one else was in the lunchroom except Marcia, who looked so helpless . . . friendless. She teeter-tottered down the aisle, trying to balance her tray in one hand and an open book in the other. Tess forced her foot out into the aisle. Out of the corner of her eye, she saw Erin smile at her as Erin lifted her milk to her mouth. Tess paused for a second, then, almost too late, pulled her foot back in.

Marcia passed, and Tess looked longingly at the Coronado Club table. Lauren flipped her hair and leaned over to the next table where Andrea sat. She whispered something to Andrea, who nodded. Andrea stuck her foot way, way out into the aisle. Marcia was busy reading her book and didn't realize anything was happening until her spaghetti exploded into the air, falling into her hair. The tray crashed to the floor and milk splashed all over Marcia's shirt. Clattering silverware jumped like frogs on the floor.

The lunch monitor hurried over to Marcia to help

her clean up. The lunchroom echoed with laughter as one student after another howled at the crying Marcia. Spaghetti stuck all over the place, including inside her book. No one noticed as Andrea stood, picked up her tray, and moved to the Coronado Club table. No one except Tess, that is. Colleen gave Tess a disapproving glare then turned away. Lauren put her arm around Andrea. Tess couldn't take any more, so she turned back around in her chair.

"That was really mean," Erin said. "Some people just don't have a clue."

Tess sat quietly in her chair. After a minute she answered, "Yeah, you're right." It *was* mean. In spite of her sadness over Colleen, she was glad she had pulled her foot back. As she stood up, her necklace caught on a loop of fabric in her shirt, and an edge of the charm dug into her flesh. "Let's go," Tess said.

Erin stood up, and they walked outside. As they walked by the Coronado Club table, Tess heard Lauren whisper, "You're a bigger chicken than these blobs they serve for lunch." Tess pretended not to hear or to notice that Colleen didn't look at her. *So much for Lauren's party tonight.*

ten

Tom

Saturday, September 14

Tess had consoled herself with the thought that she had the party to go to on Saturday and then surprised herself by how much she was enjoying it.

Cupping her hands around her mouth, Erin shouted, "Pull harder on the left rein."

Tess grasped the tough leather strap in her left hand and gave it a good yank. Immediately, Solomon turned left, and Tess looked back over her shoulder to smile at Erin.

Erin smiled back. She mounted Dustbuster and rode up to Tess's side. "You're doing great for someone who has only ridden a few times. You seem really natural."

"Thanks," Tess said. "Even though I haven't been around horses much, I like them a lot." She patted Solomon's silky coat. It felt like the tassels on top of fresh-picked corn. The beautiful horse had white socks about an eighth of the way up each leg while the rest of his coat was the color of milk chocolate. Tess urged him to go faster, and his feet trampled the reddish desert soil while the wind tossed tumbleweeds around as if they were beachballs.

For at least an hour the girls circled around the corral, finally venturing out into the open acres around the property.

"Are you sure I'm ready for this?" Tess asked her friend, a little nervous at riding into the open.

"Sure I am. I wouldn't let you go if I didn't think so. I've known Solomon practically my whole life, and he'll take care of you."

The horses gentled to a walk, and Erin pulled Dustbuster up alongside Tess. "What do you think of the place?"

"I love it. Do you come here often?"

"Yeah, almost every weekend. It depends on what else is going on. Now that my brother's basketball season has started, we'll probably come by less."

"I'd like to come with you some other time . . . ," Tess said. Her voice trailed off as she became a little embarrassed at inviting herself over.

Erin smiled her big, genuine smile. "That would be great. Jessica is a little afraid of horses, so I don't have many friends to ride with. Hmm." Her smile faded a bit. "Look over there."

"Looks like a monsoon is coming," Tess said after glancing at the sky. Fat black clouds grumbled in the distance, eating up the blue sky as they traveled closer and closer.

"We'd better finish before it starts to rain. Ready to settle for a short ride?" Erin led the way back toward the corral. Tess followed, enjoying the quiet. Slowing Dustbuster to a walk, Erin indicated for Tess to do the same with her mount. The horses sauntered back to the house, where Erin's mom had been keeping a close eye on the girls.

"I'm really sorry Jessica couldn't come," Tess said. She felt bad Erin had only one girl at her party. Not even her best friend could come.

"That's okay," Erin said sadly. "Actually, Jessica might move to Seattle. Her parents are getting a divorce, and Jessica and her mom might have to live with her grandparents until her mom finds a job."

"Wow. That's too bad," Tess said.

"Nothing's for sure yet. Maybe her mom will find a job here," Erin said in a hopeful voice.

"I wish Lauren would move," Tess muttered to herself.

The girls finished the rest of the ride in silence.

"Hi, girls!" Erin's mom waved at them. "Lunch is ready. Come on in. We're having a hard time keeping Tom away from the pizza."

"Who's Tom?" Tess dismounted and rubbed Solomon's sweaty coat.

"My brother." Erin jumped off her horse, handing the reins of both horses to her Uncle Dennis, who took the mounts into the barn to care for them. The girls headed into the house.

Thick beams crisscrossed the living room ceiling. The worn wood floor was polished to a soft glow. Navajo rugs graced the walls, and large bunches of fragrant dried flowers rested in burnished brass vases throughout the great room. The curtains were drawn from the windows with twisted black cords tipped with silver. It was a ranch right out of romantic westerns.

"Hey, are we eating or what?" a boy's voice called.

"Tom, meet my friend Tess," Erin said. "Tess, this is my brother Tom."

"Hi," Tom said. At least that's what Tess thought he said. She was too busy staring at his dimpled smile, his tousled blond hair, and his strong hands gripping a basketball. He obviously was the cute boy in Erin's pictures.

Tess hadn't really liked boys too much, and she wasn't sure she actually liked this one, but she might. He looked sort of like a guy on TV, not shrimpy and annoying like sixth-grade boys.

"Don't forget me!" came a voice from beyond the couch.

"Oh, yeah. This is Josh, my little brother." Josh sat on the floor watching a movie.

"Hi, Josh."

"Can we eat now? I'm starving," Tom said as he wrestled Josh to the kitchen table in a friendly, big-brother way. That was cool. A lot of guys might treat their little brother like a bug.

"Sure," Erin's dad said. "Josh, turn off the TV. Let's gather around the table." Why were they gathering around the table?

When everyone reached out both hands and took the hand of the person to either side, Tess was confused but did the same. If she had known they were going to hold hands, she might have tried to stand next to Tom.

Instead, she sandwiched between Erin's grandpa and Josh. Everyone closed their eyes except Tess.

"Lord," Erin's dad started.

Oh, they're praying. More comfortable now that she knew what was happening, Tess closed her eyes.

"On this special day, her birthday, we want to thank you for Erin. She's a wonderful daughter, sister, and granddaughter. Bless her life this year, Lord. Help her to love and know you more deeply. Thank you for providing this food. In Jesus' name we pray. Amen." Everyone unclasped hands and looked at each other.

"Erin, why don't you and Tess serve yourselves first? Then we'll follow," Erin's mom said.

"If there's anything left," Josh commented. Just like Tyler.

Most of the birthday party time was spent riding, then eating, but the girls had a little time afterward, too. Erin suggested they play Clue, and Josh and Tom joined them. Tess sneaked a peak at Tom, and he smiled back at her. He didn't seem to think he was too mature to play with them, and he was really nice to Erin. After two games, a familiar honk sounded outside. The rain was pouring now, so Tess figured her mom didn't want to get drenched. "I have to go, Erin. My mom's here."

Erin's mother drew back the curtain from the window and waved toward the car. Erin saw Tess to the door. "Thanks for coming and for the CD. It was fun riding together. We'll have to do it more often."

"I had a good time," Tess said, surprised by the truth.

"I'd like to come back. Let's talk about it next week at school."

"Okay." Erin opened the door. "See you later."

Tess dashed out to the car, soaked by the time she got in, and sat down.

"It's pouring all over the valley," her mom said. "A couple of roads are flooded out. We'll have to take it slow." The roads often flooded during the Arizona monsoons. "Did you have a good time?"

"Yeah, I did. Erin's horses were great. I rode pretty fast, and I didn't fall or anything. Also, her grandparents' house was very 'old West,' just like in the movies. I'm sort of hungry, though. Her brothers ate most of the pizza before I could get back for seconds. Her mom offered me something else, but I felt kind of funny and said no."

"I'm glad you enjoyed yourself. You'll have to invite Erin over sometime."

"Okay," said Tess. "She's more fun than I thought she would be."

The two rode together in silence.

"Tess . . ."

"Yeah?"

"I've been giving it some thought, and well, I guess you're old enough to wear dangling earrings if you want to. It's sometimes hard for me to remember you're becoming a young lady and not still my little girl." Her mom kept her eyes on the road, but Tess could see tiny tears.

"Thanks, Mom. It's okay. Don't worry about it. I

haven't been the best person in the world to deal with lately," Tess said.

The radio played softly while the windshield wipers swished back and forth across the glass, creating a comfortable sound. They rode the rest of the way home in the quiet togetherness shared by those who don't need to talk.

eleven

Unibrow

Sunday, September 15

The next night Tess could hardly believe her ears. "Colleen called," Mom hollered down the hall as Tess came out of the steamy bathroom.

"Really? Great! Thanks, Mom." Tess hurried to her room. She quickly unwrapped the towel beehived on her head and let her wet hair hang down. After combing it out, she pulled on some sweats, grabbed the phone, and dialed Colleen's number.

"Is Colleen there?" she asked after Mrs. Clark answered the phone.

"Just a minute."

"Hello?"

"Hi, Colleen. My mom said you called."

"Yeah, just a few minutes ago. Hold on while I go to my room." The phone clattered as Colleen set it down on the countertop, then picked up the other extension. "Okay, Mom, hang it up. How was your weekend?" Colleen asked.

"Fine," Tess answered. Why was Colleen talking as if nothing had happened? "How about yours?"

"Okay. Lauren's party was pretty fun. I'm sorry you weren't there, though."

"Well, yeah. I didn't know if I was still invited."

"Oh," Colleen said. "Yeah."

The silence was thick enough that Tess heard her heart pounding in her ears. Was this all Colleen was going to say? Tess twirled a strand of her damp hair around her fingers.

"I really didn't think you would trip Unibrow," Colleen finally said.

"You didn't?" Tess untwirled the strand she had just coiled up.

"No," answered Colleen. "You're too, well, good. I knew you wouldn't want to get in trouble."

"Then why did you ask me to do it?" Tess's hand tightened around the receiver.

"I'm the club president, but Lauren is actually in charge of initiation. Tripping Unibrow was Lauren's idea."

Well, that explained some things. "But you could have told her no, if you're the president," Tess said.

"Well." Colleen ignored that statement. "I talked it over with the other members Friday night, and we decided you could be in the club anyway."

"Really? With no initiation? Great!" Tess's hand relaxed.

"Well, not exactly no initiation," Colleen answered. "But we agreed to give you another chance. This time the test is something no one will know you did, and there's no way you can get in trouble."

"What is it?" Tess asked warily, her stomach tingling.

"Tomorrow is a teachers in-service day, and there's no school, right? So Tuesday, get to school a few minutes before first bell. Take a black Magic Marker, and draw a picture of Unibrow on the mirror of the girls' bathroom. You know, with a fat, black worm for eyebrows. Then write 'Marcia is a hairy unibrow' above it." Colleen snickered. "No one will know you did it."

"Yeah, but Marcia will still see it. Don't you think she feels bad enough after what Andrea did Friday?" Tess was a little indignant, although she didn't know why. She didn't even know Marcia.

"Tess, please do this. I really want you to be in the club. Aren't we good friends?" Colleen pleaded.

"I guess so," Tess whispered. She noticed Colleen hadn't said "best friends."

"Then come on. The others all had to be initiated, so they won't let you be in the club unless you are, too. I can't change the rule. Lauren was totally mad when I asked. Don't worry about Marcia. We'll make it up to her. Maybe invite her to a party or something. She'll think she's cool. That will make it okay."

Tess could tell by Colleen's pleading tone of voice that she wanted Tess to join the Coronado Club. And Tess wanted to. Colleen was a lot of fun, and so were the others, except Lauren, who probably didn't want Tess in the club anyway. Maybe Marcia wouldn't even be in school on Tuesday. If she was, maybe they could make it up to her by inviting her to some parties. Tess would make sure they didn't blow it off, that Marcia got invited. Marcia would never have the chance to hang out with the in-crowd otherwise.

"Okay," Tess said.

"Great! I'd better go. My mom's calling. See you Tuesday." Colleen clicked off.

Tess stared at the phone in her hand for a minute until the dial tone returned, then she gently placed the phone back on the receiver. She pushed herself off the floor to open her door, planning to kiss her parents good night.

She stopped halfway down the hall, hearing loud voices. "Well, do you want me to go alone? Tell them my wife is too busy to visit with them?"

"Don't you think they'll understand that your wife works, too?" Her mom's voice trembled with anger. "I have things to do, too, you know, and I carry more than my share of the housework."

"No one said you don't. But I carry more than half of the income, and I could use your support tomorrow night," her dad answered. His voice was not as loud but just as angry.

"Fine. We'll go to Pinnacle Peak. But if I miss my deadline, who's going to explain that?" Mom stomped toward the hall, and Tess scurried into her room before they met.

"Oh, boy," Tess muttered. Her parents hardly ever disagreed, but when they did, it made Tess nervous.

She wondered if this was how Jessica's parents acted before the divorce. What if Tess's parents were going to divorce, too?

Tess closed her door and walked to her desk.

Dear Diary,

I don't have much to say tonight. The good news is I can still be in the club. The bad news is I have to get Marcia after all. Good night, Diary. I'll write more tomorrow.

She logged off before slipping into bed. The sheets rustled crisp and cool against her skin. Her mom must have changed them today. Tess's hand reached under the lampshade and flicked off the light. She leaned forward and pressed her chin against her bent knees. As she stared out her window, a star shot across the inky sky. Tess wished on it. "I wish my parents would make up. I wish Marcia wouldn't come to school on Tuesday."

Do wishes come true? she wondered. *How about prayers? Does God really answer prayers? Erin's family seems to think so, and so does Janelle. Janelle pretty much knows everything.*

"God," Tess whispered, "I miss Colleen. I finally have a friend, a best friend, which I didn't have all last year after the move. Moving wasn't my idea, remember, even though I know Mom and Dad were thinking it would be great. I want to be popular, and I deserve to be popular just as much as Andrea and Melody, even if I don't play touch football or have dimples. I deserve it more than Lauren, for sure. But I don't want to hurt Marcia. The good thing, though, is if I am in the Coronado Club, I can invite Marcia to parties and stuff, sort of make it up to her. Don't you think that will make it worthwhile? Isn't it how things end up that matters?" Tess sat silently, waiting for God to answer. Nothing seemed to happen.

She looked out over the backyard, noticing the pool lights were on. Tonight, as it did every night, the cleaning tube snaked around and around the inside of the pool cleaning off the day's almost invisible buildup of slime.

"Help me, God, if you are there," Tess prayed toward the sky. "Somehow tell me what to do." She lay back in bed, wandering between consciousness and sleep.

twelve

Not Even Janelle

Monday, September 16

Tess rested for a minute on the lawn chair after spending her day off in the backyard, edging the small patch of grass and trimming the azaleas. She heard her mother call, "Come on in, Tess. You've been in the sun long enough." Tess unstuck herself from the chair and headed to the pool, slipping into the water once more to cool off before going into the house.

She figured she had better put on some lotion. Her skin, stretched taut and dry from the chlorine, flaked. A big beach towel hugged her waist like a skirt, tucked in at the top and covering her stomach. Once in the kitchen she pulled a cold soda from the fridge and sat down at the table with some chips and salsa. "Where are you guys going tonight?" she mumbled, as a piece of chip fell out of her mouth. She plucked it from her bathing suit, putting the chip on the table.

"Pinnacle Peak Patio," her mom answered, "with Dad's out-of-town guests from work."

"I thought you weren't going," Tess said, trying to sound casual.

"Why ever would you think that?" her mom asked, looking surprised.

"I heard you and Dad arguing last night."

"Tess, you shouldn't listen to other people's conversations," she chided.

"Well, then you shouldn't have a fight in the family room. I was coming out to say good night, that's all. It's not as if I was trying to eavesdrop or anything." Tess felt defensive. It was her house, too, after all.

"You're right," said her mom. "But it wasn't a fight. Dad was tired and worried about a big account, and I was tired and worried about a deadline. The stress got the best of us. What you didn't hear were our apologies later and our agreement to work out the situation for the best for both of us."

"Oh," Tess said.

"It's a normal thing for married people to disagree, Tess."

"I thought people who argued got a divorce."

"Honey, there's a lot more to divorce than that. And Dad and I are definitely not getting a divorce."

"Oh. I wish I could come tonight," Tess said, changing the subject. "I love Pinnacle Peak, even if it is kind of touristy." The rustic restaurant, a big ranch, sat on a mountain crest. Most of the tables were picnic planks set outdoors on a "patio" that held several hundred people. Huge open grills charbroiled thick steaks, and billowy mesquite clouds floated into the air.

"Remember when we took Grandma and Grandpa Thomas?" Tess giggled, and her mom joined her.

"Yes, I'll never forget the look on Mother Thomas's face."

The family had taken Tess's grandparents to the restaurant, and everyone but Grandpa dug into the steaks partnered with tender cornbread, smoky cowboy beans, and lots of other fixings saddled alongside. Grandpa waited patiently, tapping his toes to the live country music while his "well done" steak order was grilled. When the waitress showed up with a boot on his plate, Tyler laughed so hard he nearly choked, but Grandma didn't think it was funny. The waitress finally did serve Grandpa his real dinner.

"Remember when Dad brought the Japanese visitors and one wore a tie?" Tess's mom said, and they both laughed louder.

"Yes. Dad warned his visitors this time—no ties allowed!" The restaurant had a special necktie policy. If anyone wore one, the waitress clipped it off and then tied it to the rafters inside. Thousands of cut ties hung there, attesting to a long history of enforced casual wear.

"Dad did make sure Mr. Kawamoto received a new tie." Mrs. Thomas wiped her eyes, moist from laughing so hard, before continuing. "Janelle is coming over. She'll be here in about an hour. I thought it might be fun for you to have her as company." Janelle was sixteen and lived down the street. Tess thought she was absolutely the best. She had gorgeous, strawberry-blonde hair and drove an old two-seater convertible. She never treated Tess like a little kid but talked to her as if she were an equal. In some ways, Tess considered Janelle more of an older sister than a baby-sitter.

"Great," Tess answered. "What's for dinner?"

"Pizza. I know you just had it at Erin's the other day, but I already promised Tyler."

"No problem. I can always eat more pizza."

"Good. I'll leave cash with Janelle. She can order it as soon as we leave." Mom wiped her hands on a dish-towel and left the room. A few minutes later, Tess heard the shower water running, so she figured Mom was getting ready.

Tess grabbed a book, *A Wrinkle in Time,* and walked back out to the patio. After dragging a chair into the shady area, she opened her book to where she had left off. She must have been reading for quite a while, be-cause the next thing she knew her mom and dad were calling good-bye. A few minutes later Janelle came out.

"Hi, Tess, how's it going?" Janelle smiled at Tess.

"Okay, I guess. Where's Tyler?"

"In the house. He's watching TV until the pizza ar-rives. How's sixth grade? Did you get 'The Frog'?"

"No, I'm happy to say. I have a new teacher, Ms. Martinez. She lets us have a lot of freedom."

"That's cool," Janelle said. "Are your friends in there, too? Like, um, what was her name? Colleen?"

"Well, no. She's in Mr. Basil's class. Along with every-one else."

"Oh," said Janelle, pulling up a chair. "How's that going?"

"Okay, I guess." After a minute Tess asked, "Janelle, were your friends in the 'in' group when you were in sixth grade?"

"Some were and some weren't," Janelle answered. "Why?"

"Well, when you were in sixth grade, was it important to be popular? Did you have a lot of friends?"

"I had some friends in sixth grade, not a bunch," Janelle said. "I wasn't friends with the really popular girls because they were sort of bossy. It didn't matter to me because my best friend wasn't in the really popular group."

"That's what I'm afraid of," Tess said, more to herself. "My best friend is popular." Then she asked, "Was it important in seventh grade to be popular? Is it important in high school?"

"Well, it's sometimes easier if you are popular, Tess," Janelle answered. "It seems as if more people like and respect you, and you're in on everything. Sometimes it's not easier. Sometimes there is a lot of pressure to do things to stay popular, like dress a certain way or not get good grades. Is that what you mean?"

"Not really," Tess said. Ho-hum, not even Janelle understood.

"Pizza's here," Tyler called from the house.

Janelle stood up. "I'd better go pay. But remember, Tess, it's important to have friends you can be yourself with. Friends you can be goofy, sad, and honest with. Friends who like you exactly as you are and encourage you to be yourself. If you make a friend like that, she's a good friend. If she's popular, great. If she's not, that's okay, too." Janelle walked toward the house to pay for the pizza. "Let's go eat."

Tess wished she were as confident as Janelle, that she had a sixth-grade friend like her. She sighed. Yet not even Janelle truly understood. Tess unwound the towel from her waist and pulled on an oversized Mickey Mouse T-shirt. She sat outside for a few minutes and let the evening breeze caress her warm skin. The crickets started up again, chirping in their mysterious code.

Better go and get a piece of pizza. She would need all the strength she could get for tomorrow.

Multiple Choice

Tuesday, September 17

Tomorrow came soon enough.

"Mom, I have to go to school early today." Tess grabbed her backpack from the kitchen floor. "Can you ask Tyler to walk with Big Al?"

"Sure, Tess. What's up?"

"Oh, nothing." Tess fidgeted, looking at the floor. "I just need to do something early, that's all."

"Okay, honey. Just don't hang around outside the school. Go right in and do your work, okay?"

It'll be work, all right. Tess sat down at the breakfast table, unzipping her backpack. Math book, Mexico report, folder. Rummaging around, she searched for something she had put in there last night, finally finding it. A permanent black marker. She fingered it for a minute before returning it to the pack's bottom and zipping the pack closed.

Morning light glinted off the pretty glass bowl of fruit and yogurt her mom set at Tess's place. Tess picked up her fork to poke at the fruit. Spearing a piece of kiwi, she took a bite. Anxiety dried out her mouth, though, and the fruit stuck first to her tongue and then caught in her throat. "I think I'll just go now." She pushed back her chair and pulled on her backpack as Tyler walked in.

"Say, old girl, where are you going so early?" he asked. "Detention?"

"No, I don't have detention," Tess snapped. Her mother stopped wiping the counter and looked at Tess.

"I don't have detention, Mom. Really." Her mom must have believed her because she turned back to the counter.

"See you," Tess called on her way out.

"Bye, honey," her mom said.

"Yeah, 'Bye, honey,'" Tyler mimicked as Tess slammed the door shut.

The day grew comfortably warm as the sun hiked higher and higher up the McDowell Mountains. Tess shuffled down the street, wishing she were already grown up and didn't have to go to school every day. "I'm sick of following rules. I want to make my own choices," she muttered. The neighborhood woke up as the streets hummed with panting joggers and grinding garbage trucks, both consuming excess. Janelle zoomed by in her convertible and beeped at Tess. Tess waved before turning the corner to Coronado Elementary and walking up to the front door.

The sign YOU ARE BECOMING WHO YOU ARE TO BE seemed to shout to her as she entered the school. Walking to the girls' bathroom, Tess pulled open the door. A burst of lemon ammonia assaulted her nose, and she saw the paper-towel holders were stuffed, ready to begin the day. As she stared at the mirror, she figured she had better start to draw before girls came in to check their hair.

Just then she heard footsteps approaching. Tess slipped into a stall so no one would know who was in the bathroom. As she shut herself in the stall, the bathroom door opened.

"She has some unusual ideas for teaching," one voice said. The voice was nasal, sort of whiny. "She's barely out of college and thinks she's going to change the world."

That was Mrs. Lowell. Tess had had Mrs. Lowell for fifth-grade reading.

" 'Unusual' is not the word I would use! 'Undisciplined' would be a better choice. Her students will never respect her. I know I don't!" the other voice answered.

Who were they talking about?

"Have you heard about the units she chose for science and technology? And the clothes she wears . . ." Mrs. Lowell's voice again. "I'd never wear lipstick if my lips were that big. And that turquoise and silver hair clip—she wears it every day! Maybe she should cut off her hair if she can't think of anything else to do with it."

They were talking about Ms. Martinez! A purse clasp snapped, echoing through the bathroom; the door squeaked open, then eased shut. Footsteps grew faint as the two teachers walked farther away. Tess sat still for a minute.

They don't even know Ms. M. The class does so respect her, because she respects them. Her hair clip is pretty, and nobody ever mentioned her lips. Anyway, don't they have anything better to do than to make Ms. M. look bad? Tess knew Ms. Martinez would be hurt if she knew what Mrs. Lowell and the other teacher had been saying.

After another minute Tess decided she had better complete her drawing before anyone else came in. She walked over to the mirror.

After pulling out her marker, Tess zipped up her backpack and hoisted it onto her back so she could make a quick escape. She took a deep breath. Before she could change her mind, she drew a thick, black circle for the face.

Don't you have anything better to do than to make Marcia look bad? she thought. Startled, she realized they were the exact words she had been thinking about Mrs. Lowell. The image of Marcia in the lunchroom on Friday with spaghetti in her hair, crying in front of the whole school, stood out vividly in Tess's mind. Maybe this was the answer Tess had asked for. She stood, eye to eye with her reflection in the mirror, her face framed by the big black circle she had drawn. Then she capped the marker and put it into her pack. Nervously, she straightened her hair in the mirror before going to class. She didn't wait outside Mr. Basil's class today to say hi to Colleen. Tess couldn't face her.

Several hours later the lunch bell rang. Ms. M. signaled to the class to put away their books and papers in preparation for lunch. For the tenth time Tess wondered where Erin was. Of all the days for her not to be

here! Now Tess would have to sit alone at lunch. She
knew that Colleen and the rest of the Coronado Club
would have realized by now that Tess hadn't completed
her initiation. She was out of the club forever and for
sure this time.

Walking down the hallway to the lunchroom, Tess
kept her eyes straight ahead. After piling fries and a
cheeseburger on her tray, she sat down. Marcia was in
line. She had real guts to show up at school today.
Marcia sat next to another girl and started talking to
her, and the girl laughed.

Great. Even Marcia had friends, someone to sit with.
After finishing her burger, Tess placed her tray on the
dish return. She took her paperback outside with her
and sat alone. Fifth grade all over again.

Tess had settled into her book, sitting cross-legged
on the ground, when a burst of laughter followed by
snickering shot across the courtyard, and Tess looked
up. Over in the corner were Melody, Andrea, Lauren,
and Colleen. They had their heads together but kept
glancing at Tess, laughing. Andrea put her hands together so they resembled a book and pretended to
read. The other three started to laugh again.

Tess felt her face flush with embarrassment, but she
ducked back inside her book, keeping her head down.
Don't cry, she reminded herself, *don't let them win.* But
inside she sobbed for the friend she knew she had lost,
and loneliness overcame her.

fourteen

True Reflection

Wednesday, September 18

Tess felt somewhat better the next day and was even able to finish all her math problems before the rest of the class. Ho-hum. She chewed her pencil eraser, wishing everyone else would hurry up so they could get on with the next set of problems. Ms. Martinez's pen scratched as she corrected papers. At least if Erin were here Tess could write a note or something. Jessica hadn't come back to school yet, either. Tess wondered if they were somewhere together.

Splat! A spitball stung Tess's arm. She was disgusted to think someone else's spit had touched her skin. Glancing over her shoulder she spied Scott Shearin smirking behind his textbook. Tess felt the immediate need to wash off her arm. She raised her hand, and Ms. M. glanced over the top of her glasses. Her pen stopped scratching on the paper in front of her.

"Miss Thomas? You have a question?"

Tess watched Scott's eyes widen in alarm. Would she tattle?

"Uh, yes. May I go to the rest room?"

"Certainly." Ms. M. handed Tess a pass, then lowered her head to her task again.

Tess smiled as Scott breathed a sigh of relief. She walked toward the door and then down the hallway to the bathroom. The hinges complained loudly as she pulled open the door to the familiar blast of lemon ammonia.

Tess gasped as she faced the mirror. Blood rushed through her neck and into her head, pressing against her eyeballs. The circle she had drawn yesterday had been transformed into a complete face with crossed eyes and a crooked mouth. Worst of all were the huge ears with the word "Dumbo" written in one and "Flyers" in the other. Underneath someone had scrawled, "Mirror, Mirror, on the wall, who's the biggest geek of all? Tess Thomas!"

Tess turned around and grasped for a stall as acid filled her throat. The ceiling circled the stall as if in orbit, and she couldn't get a deep breath. She rested on the toilet seat. After a few minutes, the acid slunk back into her stomach and the room slowed down, but hot tears still splashed her cheeks. Unlike yesterday, Tess couldn't will herself not to cry. The Coronado Club, of course! But which one drew this? Lauren? Andrea?

Then she remembered, and the memory hit her like a baseball bat in the gut. The only person who had heard her called "Dumbo Flyers" last summer was

Colleen. Tess couldn't believe it. Not Colleen! Just a few weeks ago, Tess would have defended her friend to anyone, certain Colleen would have done the same for her. And now Colleen had turned on her.

Was Colleen always such a backstabber but Tess had been too blind to see it? Or had Colleen changed? Tess was embarrassed by the thought that other people would see this drawing. Mostly her chest ached at the thought of betrayal by someone who, just this morning, was her best friend. Tess blew her nose on a thin piece of toilet paper and threw it in the toilet before leaving the stall.

She twisted on the water faucet, letting it run as hot as it could while she balled up and soaked several paper towels. After wringing them out, she scrubbed the ugly drawing on the mirror, finally scraping at it in frustration with her fingernails. Nothing happened. It was permanent. Tess slammed the paper towel balls into the garbage and gazed into her reflection.

On one half of the mirror, the ugly drawing stirred up hurt all over again. The other half of the glass revealed her true reflection: red nose, puffy cheeks, big ears. Glancing first at one reflection, then the other, Tess stared at herself, remembering what she had not done yesterday. Marcia could have been standing here instead, crying and feeling sick. Tess imagined Marcia with red nose and puffy cheeks, staring into the mirror at a caricature of herself with a fat unibrow.

Sniffing with satisfaction, Tess was glad she had not made Marcia feel this awful. Nothing could have made up for it, not parties, not fake friends, nothing. Tess recalled the conversation she had overheard between Mrs. Lowell and the other teacher. Maybe Colleen would grow up to be like Mrs. Lowell; Lauren would for sure. Tess snatched a new paper towel out of the dispenser, balled it up, and flung it at the ugly drawing before leaving the bathroom.

As Tess walked into the classroom, Ms. M. motioned for her student to come to her desk. "Are you all right? I was starting to worry."

Grateful that the teacher did not accuse her of slacking off but instead showed concern, Tess decided to talk with her. She probably couldn't hold her hurt in, anyway.

"Can I talk with you outside the room, please?" Tess asked.

Ms. M. took one look at Tess's puffy eyes and agreed. Once out in the hall Tess found it difficult to talk without the tears starting again. "Well, um, there's a picture in the bathroom . . . on the mirror, I mean," Tess said.

"A picture?"

"Well, a drawing, actually," Tess continued. "Of me. Making fun of me. And it says I'm a geek." The tears welled up again, brimming over her damp lids. "I tried to wash it off . . ." She couldn't continue. The tears fell too fast now.

"Don't worry, Tess. I'll ask the janitor to wash it off immediately. That way almost no one will have had a chance to see it."

"You will? Thank you." Tess dabbed her eyes with the tissue Ms. M. pulled from her pocket.

"Can you go back to class?" Ms. M. asked.

"I think so. May I stay in the room for lunch, though?" She did not want to sit in the lunchroom alone today. It might be different if Erin were here.

"I think we can make an exception, due to the circumstances." Tess looked at Ms. M.'s eyes and saw they were soft. Ms. M. really did understand.

"Now, why don't you go back into class, and I'll page the janitor."

Nodding, Tess turned around and gripped the doorknob. Forcing her head up and her eyes straight ahead, she squared her shoulders and strode into the room.

fifteen

Baby Dimples

Wednesday, September 18

It took all Tess's courage to make it through the day.

"Mom, I'm home," she hollered down the hall toward her mother's office as Tess stormed into the house after school. "I'll be in my room."

Before her mom could answer, Tess ran down the hall, tightly shutting her bedroom door. The old wooden trunk her great-grandmother had brought to America squatted in the corner of Tess's room. She sat down cross-legged in front of it.

The leather straps that secured the trunk were almost worn through, and the buckle was banged up from ninety years of use. The lid opened smoothly, though, a testimony to good craftsmanship. The scents of cedar and pine rose as Tess gently lifted out her treasures. Sorting through them, she searched for one particular item. Breathing a sigh of relief, Tess lifted out Baby Dimples.

Fluffy stuffing escaped through a small hole in Baby

Dimples's arm, an arm worn through by love. Matted and ratty, Dimples's stiff hair had been styled for years by Tess and her friends. On her tenth birthday, Tess had held a special ceremony for Baby Dimples, explaining that since Tess was too old for dolls now, she would save Baby Dimples for her own daughter to love someday. Afterward, she had wrapped the doll in her soft, fuzzy, pink cotton blanket before placing Baby Dimples inside the wooden chest. Tess rarely brought out the doll, but today she needed Dimples.

With her legs pulled up to her chest, Tess clutched her doll, crying. "God," Tess prayed through her tears, "where are you? If you're really God, why do you let people do mean things that hurt other people? I tried to do the right thing, and look what happened. I'm the one who was hurt. Please, if you're there, God, help me. Answer me, help me feel better." The prayer was barely out of her mouth when Tess heard her mother knock on the door.

"Yes?" Tess called, trying to sound as if she hadn't been crying.

"May I come in?"

"Just a minute." She put Baby Dimples back inside the trunk, closed it, then leaned over to her nightstand for the box of tissues. After blowing her nose and pushing her hair back, Tess called, "Okay, you can come in now."

Her mother sat down on the bed, patting the space next to her with her hand. "Ms. Martinez called me today to tell me what happened."

"Well, don't beat around the bush or anything." Tess sniffed. Her mom reached for a couple of tissues from the box and handed one of them to Tess.

"Do you want to talk about it?"

Getting up from the floor, Tess shook her head no. She sat on the bed next to her mom. "There's nothing much to tell."

"It doesn't sound like nothing to me. From what your teacher said, it sounded pretty serious."

"It was a mean thing done by some rude girls." Tess didn't want to talk about it, but painful feelings forced the words out anyway.

"Do you know who did it?"

"Yes," Tess said, starting to cry again.

"Who?"

"Colleen and Lauren and the Coronado Club," Tess answered between sobs.

"Colleen?" Her mom gasped. "Why on earth would she do such an awful thing?"

One good thing about Tess's mom was that after she asked you a question she waited for you to answer. Even though it took Tess a few minutes, she waited quietly.

"Well, they have this club. And Colleen wanted me to be in it. I wanted to be in it, too. So they said I had to be initiated. Yesterday I was supposed to draw a mean picture of this girl on the bathroom mirror and write something bad under it."

"That's why you wanted to go in early," she said, looking stern.

"Yes, but I couldn't do it." Tess answered.

Her mom tried not to show her relief, but Tess could see it anyway.

"Well, I guess they thought I was a big chicken, because they were laughing at me during lunch yesterday. Colleen wouldn't even look at me. Then, today I had to go to the bathroom. When I got there, I saw the ugly picture of me on the mirror with crossed eyes and big ears. When I got back to the classroom, Ms. M. said she would have the janitor clean it off right away. Then I guess she called you."

Tess's mother looked as if she were about to cry herself. "How do you know it was Colleen?"

"This summer at swim team one kid told me that my ears were so big they were like Dumbo's Flyers. Colleen was the only one there from school. She knew how much it bugged me."

"Well, I'll tell you what I'm going to do," her mom said. "I'm going right now to call Mrs. Clark."

"No, no, no!" Tess waved her arms in the air. "You absolutely can't do that! Everyone will think I'm a baby. It's okay. Really, it is. I can handle it myself, Mom."

Mrs. Thomas seemed doubtful. "All right," she said at last. "But you have to do something. You realize if you don't turn them in, they will probably never be reprimanded for this."

"I know," Tess answered. "I'll take care of it myself."

After a minute her mother said, "Come here. I want to show you something." She took Tess's hands and pulled her up from the bed. "Walk over here." She led

Tess to the full-length swivel mirror. "What do you see?"

Tousled hair. Puffy eyes. Wrinkled shirt. Fat stomach. "A mess," Tess finally answered.

"I don't," said her mom. "I see someone who has the backbone to do what she knows is right. A brave girl, one who had many choices but made the right one, even though it required a big sacrifice. Take pride in knowing that you can still look yourself in the eye. I am proud to call you my daughter." She held back her tears, barely.

Tess squeaked out a grin.

"Now, I bought some frozen yogurt today. Why don't you treat yourself? I need to start dinner. Your dad will be home soon." She opened the door.

"Okay," Tess answered. "Mom, please don't say anything to Dad, all right? I don't really want to talk about this anymore."

Her mom kissed the top of Tess's head. As she turned to leave, something pink and fuzzy in the corner of the room caught her eye. She smiled; it was Baby Dimples's blanket. In Tess's hurry, she had forgotten to wrap the doll back up when she put her away. She turned and winked at Tess, who blushed and smiled back.

sixteen 🌸

Secret Sisters

Friday, September 20

On Friday Ms. M. began class by saying, "I have something exciting to announce." Just then Erin walked into
the classroom, handing Ms. Martinez a pass. Ms. M.
nodded, then motioned Erin to her desk. Tess smiled
as she sat down.

"I've had a chance to review all the science project
suggestions, and I've picked a winner." Everyone
leaned forward. "Brad Anderson has proposed building
a working model of Mt. Vesuvius and the town of
Pompeii. His idea is for us to figure out the dynamics
involved in volcanoes and to duplicate them in class.
We'll study how the citizens of Pompeii were entombed
and learn about the archaeological digs that found the
remains of the city. This is an excellent idea," Ms. M.
continued, "and I think a winning idea. Congratula-
tions, Brad." Brad's face flushed red, but he smiled.

Tess turned and grinned at him but was secretly

disappointed she hadn't won. Science was her strongest subject.

At least Joann hadn't won. She was very smart, and she knew it. Her dad was smart, too, and she wanted everyone else to know that. Actually, Joann thought she knew everything. Tess had to admit that Joann did have pretty black hair, which glistened in shiny, beaded cornrows.

"Please choose a partner to work with for the duration of the project, then return to your seats, and open up your math books," Ms. Martinez continued.

Tess leaned across the row to Erin. "Want to be partners for the science project?"

Erin answered. "Sure! But I'm not very smart in science."

"Oh, well, that's okay," said Tess, not knowing what else to say. "Where have you been?"

"I had strep throat, and I couldn't come back to school until today."

"I hope you're feeling better," Tess said.

Ms. Martinez called the class to attention, and they opened their math books. Tess worked on the problems for a few minutes before scribbling to Erin, "My mom is taking me out to lunch tomorrow." Rolling up the note, Tess stuffed it inside a big, fat pen. She passed the pen to Erin, who laughed, then opened it up, plucking out the note.

After reading it, Erin wrote back, "Cool! Your mom sounds great." She passed the note back to Tess.

"Most of the time she is," Tess wrote. "Anyway, she

said after lunch I could take a friend with me to the mall if I wanted. Do you want to come?" She put the note back inside the pen and passed it to Erin.

"I'll ask my mom," Erin scribbled, "and call you tonight." She passed it back and went to work on her math, frowning. Erin still had almost half the problems to complete.

At lunch that day Tess sat down across from Erin. Yum, submarine sandwiches and carrot sticks were on the menu. Tess's mouth watered. The sub rolls were soft and fresh, still smelling of yeast and flour. Spicy vinaigrette bathed each half of the roll while colorful layers of Italian cold cuts, cheeses, ripe tomatoes, and crisp lettuce crowded in between.

"Where's Jessica?" Tess asked as Erin bit into her sandwich.

Erin swallowed what was in her mouth before lamenting, "Jessica won't be here anymore. Her mom found a job, and they are moving to Seattle for sure. They'll be back for a few days to pack, but then they're gone."

"I'm sorry," Tess said. "I know you were best friends."

"Yeah, I guess we'll write. I might visit her over Christmas break. Hey, why don't you sit with them anymore?" Erin jerked her thumb toward the Coronado Club table.

"Um, long story," Tess answered, shifting in her seat. She wasn't up to telling Erin about what had happened Wednesday. She would find out about it soon enough.

Erin bit into her cherry cobbler. "You know, the food here isn't so bad."

"I don't know how you stay skinny when you eat so much."

"That's what my brother Tom says," Erin answered as she took another bite.

"Do you think your brother will be home when I come to pick you up tomorrow?"

"I don't know. Why?" Erin asked, looking at Tess as if she were weird.

"Well," Tess said, "actually, I think he's sort of cute."

"Cute? Oh gross! You have bad taste in boys, Tess. He smells like he's been playing basketball, which he almost always has been."

"I didn't notice," Tess said. "If you want to talk about gross, you should live with my eight-year-old brother, Tyler, for a week. He's obnoxious, and his friend Big Al's great ambition in life is to be in the Belching Hall of Fame."

"Don't forget, I have an eight-year-old brother, too. I'm smooshed right between them. Actually, I've always wanted a sister," Erin confided.

"Me, too," Tess said. "I think it would be so cool to have a sister, maybe even a twin. It would be like having a best friend for life."

"Do you know what would be fun? To pretend we are sisters. You know, Secret Sisters. Like, maybe even at the mall tomorrow, if I can go."

"We don't look anything alike!" Tess said, laughing. But it did sound like a good idea.

"That's okay. Lots of twins don't look alike. They aren't all identical. Maybe you look like our dad and I look like our mom. It would be fun to pretend at the mall and see how many people we can fool." Erin finished off her sub.

"Okay, let's do it," Tess said. "I could use some fun in my life. Let's go outside." They both stood up and rambled toward the open area.

Tess glanced at Colleen when she passed the Coronado Club table, remembering her promise to her mother to do something about Colleen being so mean. Tess guessed she should talk to her. Maybe after school. No, today her mom was picking them up for Tyler's piano lesson. Monday after school, for sure, when Colleen was alone. Just ask her why she did it, then walk away.

seventeen

Girls' Day Out

Saturday, September 21

Before Tess had to face Monday, though, and an encounter with Colleen, Tess savored her fabulous Saturday out with her mother.

"Mom," breathed Tess as she spun around to absorb the restaurant's atmosphere, "this place is absolutely gorgeous!" The ceiling was high, maybe three stories. Huge picture windows framed gardens lush with gnarled orange trees and soft ferns. Buttery yellow linen drapes, richly dotted with wildflowers, were pulled back with ornate brass swags.

"Two for lunch?" The maître d' asked.

"Yes, we have reservations for Thomas," Tess's mom answered.

"Right this way." His crisp black suit rustled slightly as he wove through the dining room, finally arriving at their table. "Here we are, ladies. Your waiter will be with you shortly." As soon as he had seated them and left, a busboy filled their water goblets from a crystal pitcher.

"This is great!" Tess said. "Look at these forks. What do we do with them all?" Silver utensils glistened; their scalloped edges matched the seashell-shaped plates set before them.

"We eat with them!" Mrs. Thomas laughed. "Let's look over the menu."

After long consideration, Tess decided on the chicken salad baked in flaky puff pastry with a salad of oranges, baby lettuce, and toasted almonds. Mom chose a minifilet lightly grilled with garlic butter and caramelized onions. "Let's order Arizona Sunsets to drink," her mom said.

"What are they?" Tess asked excitedly.

"You'll see."

The waiter took their order, and a few minutes later he placed a tall glass on a coaster in front of each of them. The liquid in the bottom of the glasses was ruby red, followed by a bright orange layer, and capped with something fizzy and clear. A long red pick skewered a cherry and an orange slice. "It's cherry syrup, orange juice, and club soda," her mother explained. She reached a long spoon into the glass and stirred. "Try it."

Tess did; it tasted wonderful. "This is a great idea, Mom," she said. "It's fun to go to lunch, you know, just us girls."

"I thought it was important for us to spend some time together. And I wanted to go somewhere special, because of, well, to help make up for the incident at school this week."

"Thanks, Mom. This is really great. And I am feeling better about the, stuff, you know, at school."

"I'm glad, honey. It's been a tough start, but I just know you're going to have a great year. Look at your new friend, Erin. What a surprise!"

"Yeah, she might turn out to be a very good friend. And I wasn't even expecting her to be!" Tess smiled, twirling a long fork between her fingers.

Her mom smiled back. "Sometimes the very best things are those you can't guess." She twirled her fork, too, as the waiter delivered their food.

After lunch, Mrs. Thomas and Tess drove to pick up Erin. "I thought we might try the new mall," her mother said, "Saguaro Center. They're supposed to have some stores that aren't at Paradise Valley Mall."

"Sounds good to me."

They pulled into Erin's driveway, and both got out so the mothers could meet. After the introductions, Tess said, "Let's go," and the three of them settled in for the drive to the mall. Mrs. Thomas gunned the engine, lurching out of the driveway. The tires squealed like a dog whose tail had just been squashed. Erin looked at Tess and giggled. Tess whispered, "See, what did I tell you?" and both girls giggled again.

Once at the mall, the three of them shopped together for an hour or so before Tess's mom said, "I have a few errands to do by myself. I asked Erin's mom if it was okay if I let you guys go alone for an hour, and she said yes, so long as you don't leave the mall. Why don't you two meet me in the food court in an hour?"

"Yeah!" Tess said. "No problem. Can I have some money?"

"Don't you have any allowance left over?" Her mom frowned.

"Yes, but it's at home. I'll pay you back, I promise."

Mrs. Thomas handed her ten dollars. "Don't forget, one hour. And stay out of trouble." She raised her eyebrows, tilting her head in warning as she left.

"Let's go to Three Squared to check out earrings," Erin said.

"Okay. My mom gave me permission to wear dangly earrings. I want some like Ms. M.'s."

"Me, too," Erin said.

They walked along, talking about school, movies, and other things until they got to the trendy and cheap jewelry store. Tess scanned the selection, not finding anything.

"What are you looking for?" Erin asked.

"Hey, what about these?" Tess motioned, pointing at a charm bracelet display. "These are great! Do you have one?"

"I used to have one, but I lost it," Erin answered. "You're right. Great chains."

Tess picked out two bracelets, exactly the same. "If we're twins, we should wear matching jewelry."

"I forgot we were going to do that!" Erin laughed. "What a great idea. No one will know the bracelet is our special connection, a secret between sisters."

"Perfect," Tess said. "Let's take them." She paid, then pocketed the change.

Erin giggled. "Being sisters is fun!"

They window-shopped for a while, and Erin bought a card to send to Jessica. Then they headed toward the food court, but Mrs. Thomas hadn't arrived yet.

"Let's buy a drink." Tess said. "Do you like lemonade?"

"Yeah, I'll order," Erin said as they approached the counter. The teenage girl who waited on them straightened the hat perched on her head, a lemon-yellow beanie with a bright blue propeller.

"Can I help you?" she asked.

"Yes, we'd like two cherry lemonades," Erin said, then turned toward Tess and said, "Twins should do everything alike." Tess giggled.

"Okay, it'll be a minute," the counter girl said. After they paid for their drinks, the girls found a seat in the open area where Mrs. Thomas would be sure to see them.

"It's fun being Secret Sisters," Tess said. "Maybe we could trade clothes sometime."

"Okay," said Erin. "I love your leather vest." She chewed on her lemonade straw. "Hey, I forgot to ask you. Wednesday night at church my youth group leader told us about a huge Harvest Party we're having next month. There will be music, food, games, and a speaker. Do you want to come?"

"Will only people from your church be there, or will other people be there, too?"

"Lots of other people come. It will be fun," Erin said. "My brother's coming, too," she added slyly.

"Ha, ha," Tess said. "Okay, I'll ask my mom. Fill me in on the details later." She slurped down her drink. "Hey, there's my mom."

eighteen

She Shoots, She Scores

Monday, September 23

This wasn't going to be as easy as Tess had hoped. Beads of sweat coursed down her forehead, stinging her eyes. Monsoon season often brought muggy days like this. Her thick brown hair was matted down, and the books in her pack plastered her T-shirt to her moist skin. As she stood in front of the school, Tyler ran up to her. "Come on, Tess, I want to go home to swim."

"Can you hang out with Big Al for a little while? I'll be ready in a minute. I have to talk with someone, all right?" She gave him an expression that said, "Please give me a break."

"Yeah, okay. But hurry." Tyler lugged his books over to the third-grade hallway, trying to look big. Tess knew Colleen would be waiting in front of the school for her mom to pick her up and take her to ballet as she did every Monday. Sure enough, there was Colleen, leaning against a front wall giggling with Lauren.

Spotting Tess, Lauren turned her back. The gravel

crunched, grinding beneath Tess's feet as she approached Colleen. Adrenaline shot through her blood, making her voice tremble. "Colleen, can I talk with you for a minute? Alone?"

Shrugging her shoulders and tossing her hair, Colleen said, "Sure, why not?" She looked at Lauren. "I'll be right back." Lauren rolled her eyes and stepped aside to let Colleen pass. Colleen and Tess walked a few feet over to a shady spot under a tree. "What do you want?"

"How can you change your feelings toward me so fast?" Tess asked shakily. "Why do you hate me?"

"What makes you think I hate you?" Colleen dug her toe into the ground.

"Because of what you did. Last Wednesday."

"What are you talking about?" Colleen asked innocently.

"Don't act like you don't know," Tess exploded. "You drew that awful picture of me on the bathroom wall and wrote that I was a geek. Some best friend you turned out to be."

"No one ever said we were best friends, Tess," Colleen said coolly. "And if we were, I'm not the one who changed that. You did. Anyway, how do you know I drew the picture?"

"You're the only one who knew about my ears," Tess answered. "And you're the president of the club, so I guess you're in charge. Besides, what do you mean I changed our being best friends?" By now a small crowd was watching the heated exchange from a safe distance.

"Listen. You were a nobody, a nothing. I decided to be friends with you, introduced you to people, shared my friends with you, everything. I really liked you, Tess, because you were different. I only asked you to do one thing," Colleen continued. "And I even gave you a second chance after you wimped out of tripping Unibrow. I had to convince the other club members that you were cool and you would come through. Well, you didn't. You made me look like a fool. You brought this on yourself, Tess Thomas. So don't blame me!" Colleen started to walk back toward Lauren. A bigger crowd had gathered around by now, including Tyler.

"You're a really crummy friend," Tess called as Colleen walked away. "I'm glad I found out now before I told you any more secrets you could blab to the whole school. I'm sorry we ever met."

"Don't think I'm losing any sleep over it," Colleen called back. "You're still a nobody." She linked arms with Lauren.

Tess stood there for a few minutes; people were gawking at her.

"Come on, Tess. Let's go." Tyler pulled on her arm. She scanned the crowd. How embarrassing; everyone was staring. She looked at the ground and headed toward the street with Tyler.

"Watch out!" Tyler jumped to the sidewalk, yanking Tess with him as a car nearly ran them over. Looking up, she was shocked to see Mrs. Clark's minivan pass them and pull to a stop in front of the school.

"Bye," Lauren called as Colleen headed for the car. "I'll call you tonight to plan our next meeting."

Tess could have imagined it, but she thought Lauren was talking loudly to try to make Tess jealous. *Who cares? I don't want to be in your dumb club anyway.*

"Let's go," Tyler insisted, walking toward home. They shuffled along the two blocks home.

Tyler broke the silence. "That was really cool, Tess."

"What was?"

"Standing up to Colleen. She thinks she's the queen of the school. Everyone knows she drew that picture of you on the mirror. She might think you're a nobody, but she's a brat."

"Third graders know?" Tess was aghast.

"Yeah, so what? I'm glad you're my sister. Even if you smell." Tyler stuffed his hands in his pockets. "Come on, let's get to the pool."

"Good idea," Tess punched him on the arm, and they ran home.

As they walked up their driveway, zillions of pictures raced through Tess's mind. Colleen. The mirror. Marcia with spaghetti in her hair. Mrs. Lowell's feet. The crowd at the school.

"You're a nobody . . ." echoed in her mind.

At least this Nobody can look herself in the eye, Tess thought defensively.

She did feel better having confronted Colleen. Fingering her friendship bracelet, she drew comfort from knowing her Secret Sister would stand by her.

Later that evening Tess ate a hearty dinner for a

change. Afterward, she helped her mom load the dishwasher, then said, "I'm going to my room for a while. Call me when you guys put in the movie." Her mom loved old movies. Tonight they had rented *Casablanca*.

"Why don't you clean up your room while you're in there?"

Yeah, yeah. Tess opened her door and walked in.

It was pretty messy. Hangers were scattered all over the room like downed electrical wires, and wads of paper, crumpled rejects from last week's homework, lay strewn on the carpet like old popcorn balls. It had been ages since she had cleaned her fishbowl, and Goldy was gasping for air at the top of the slimy green water. She'd clean it tonight for sure. Tess popped in a CD.

"I feel pretty good right now, God," she said aloud. She stopped, surprised to find herself praying. Is that all praying was? Talking? As she picked up some clothes from the floor, something clinked to the ground.

The necklace. Tess bent over and fingered the "Forever Friends" necklace Colleen had given her last summer. Tess had taken it off to go swimming a few days ago and had never put it back on. Too bad Colleen didn't really mean the "forever" part. Tess opened her jewelry box and watched the ballerina dance, swirling in her pink gauze tutu, knowing nothing of the sadness that sometimes came with real people's lives. Lucky dancer. Just as Tess was about to drop the necklace into the box, she changed her mind. "She shoots, she scores!" Tess tossed the necklace, and it banked off the rim of the algae-infested fishbowl before plopping in.

She smiled and turned on her computer, uncapping her lip gloss while she waited for her program to appear. Smoothing the gloss on her lips, she wrote,

Dear Diary,

Much too much to write all that has happened, but I promise you it's good. I do miss Colleen, at least the old Colleen, but I'm not sure the old Colleen was ever real. Anyway, we're not best friends now, not even friends really. But I feel okay about that. My feelings aren't hurt so much anymore. Even Tyler was proud of me, for a minute anyway. He'll be back to normal tomorrow, I'm sure.

And I didn't hurt Marcia. I'm not going to be a Mrs. Lowell when I grow up. I do have a friend, after all, and I think she'll be a real friend. One like Janelle said, who likes me just as I am and encourages me to be myself. She's my Secret Sister (I'll explain later). Her name is Erin, and she invited me to a party at her church.

Tess accidentally kicked her big toe into the bottom desk drawer.

Oh yeah, gotta go, Diary. Important business to take care of.

Love, Tess

Tess signed off and reached into the bottom drawer, pulling out her fifth-grade class picture. She stared at the snapshot of herself, then glanced in the mirror. She seemed different, more mature maybe. Definitely not so sad. Tess set down the picture for a minute. She picked up a paper from her desk, one Ms. Martinez had stuck a smiley-face sticker on and had written "100%! Good Job!" Carefully, so as not to lose the sticky part, Tess peeled the sticker off the paper. She gently laid it onto the class picture, resting the smiley face next to last year's sad face. This year was definitely *not* fifth grade all over again.

"Tess," she heard her mother call, "Erin is on the phone."

Have More Fun!!

Visit the official website at:
www.secretsisters.com

There are lots of cool activities, exciting things to do with your own secret sisters, games, updates, a photo gallery, and other great stuff. Be the first to know when new books are released! See you there today!

If you would like to write to me, please send mail to:

Sandra Byrd
P.O. Box 2115
Gresham, OR 97030

Arizona Sunsets

You and your sis can enjoy an Arizona Sunset together, no matter where you live! Just mix up the following and enjoy!

You'll need:

Two large, clear glasses
One can of 7-Up, Sprite, etc.
One cup of orange juice
Large jar of maraschino cherries
Measuring cups and spoons

Pour 3/4 cup of 7-Up into each glass. Wait till it has settled, then add 1/2 cup of orange juice to each. Let settle again.

Grab some measuring spoons, and measure out 2 tablespoons of the cherry liquid from the jar of maraschino cherries. Carefully pour down the inside rim of one glass, then repeat with the next.

Let settle and enjoy!

Solve this puzzle for exciting clues to what you'll read inside Book Two!

Across

1 Under the big top
5 Caring for children
6 Nicknamed "Mango"
7 Small horses
9 A "bone"-ified person
12 Reaping what you sow
13 Bad situation

Down

1 Fowl meal
2 Female siblings
3 Lobe pendants
4 A girl's "best friend"
8 Pardon
10 Missing
11 Postal deliveries
13 Heartthrob

#8 *Petal Power:* Ms. Martinez is the most beautiful bride in the world, and the sisters are there to help her get married. When trouble strikes her honeymoon plans, Tess and Erin must find a way to help save them.

The Secret Sister Handbook: 101 Cool Ideas for You and Your Best Friend! It's fun to read about Tess and Erin and just as fun to do things with your own Secret Sister! This book is jampacked with great things for you to do together all year long.

Available March 2000:

#9 *First Place:* The Coronado Club insists Tess won't be able to hike across the Grand Canyon and plans to tell the whole sixth grade about it at Outdoor School. Tess looks confident but worries in silence, not wanting to share the secret that could lead to disaster.

#10 *Camp Cowgirl:* The Secret Sisters are ready for an awesome summer camp at a Tucson horse ranch, until something—and someone—interferes. What happens if your best friend wants other friends, and you're not sure, but you might too?

Available September 2000:

#11 *Picture Perfect:* Tess and Erin sign up for modeling school—and get their first assignment! But when they show up, they find out that things aren't always what we expect, a fact confirmed when Tess's mother has her baby.

#12 *Indian Summer:* When Tess and Erin sign up to go on their first mission trip—to the Navajo reservation—they plan to teach vacation Bible school. As often happens, they end up learning more than they teach, and Tess has the most important experience of her new Christian life.